CORPS OF SILENCE

By

Julie D'Olympio

Copyright © 2021 by Julie D'Olympio

All rights reserved

Printed in the United States of America

ISBN 978-0-578-31442-6

LCCN 2021921837

Chapter One

August 15, 2018.

Japan 9:15 P.M.

Captain Arthur Blake had just landed his jet at the Marine Corps hanger in Iwakuni, Japan. He was advance party on a six-month deployment. He was a handsome man, 27, with dark brown hair and hazel eyes. He promised Sara, his wife, that he would call her as soon as he arrived. His flight was long and he was tired, but he was anxious to get to his hotel to call her. Taking his helmet off, Arthur looked around.

It was dark out, but there was lots of light coming from the hangar nearby. He was excited to be in Japan.

He hated being away from Sara without being able to call her, but he knew she would be okay since she had other military wives to spend time with. Plus, his pilot buddies; Second Lieutenant O'Riley, First Lieutenant Stevens and First Lieutenant Quinn were back at home to keep an eye on her for him. He missed her and was looking forward to her voice over the phone. Arthur started climbing down the ladder out of the cockpit when a military policeman and a chaplain approached him. He didn't know why they would be approaching him except for bad news. He had been having a weird feeling all evening, but just thought it was his excitement about going to Japan. As soon as he saw the two men, he took a step back and propped himself against the ladder.

"Don't tell me I'm illegally parked." He chuckled a little nervously. The chaplain spoke up with a straight face.

"Captain Arthur Blake, would you come with us please? We need to speak with you about your wife Sara." Arthur just stood there. He immediately felt sick. Arthur didn't know what to say.

"Sara, is she okay?" He looked back at the Chaplain. "What's going on?" The chaplain looked down but didn't speak. After a brief pause, the MP spoke up.

"There's been an accident." he said. "You'll need to come with us and we'll tell you what we know." The world stopped. The breeze that was just blowing seemed to just freeze. Life became unreal. Arthur couldn't believe what was happening. She had to be okay.

"Just tell me, please! Is Sara okay? Tell me!" The chaplain put his hand on Arthur's shoulder.

"Last night your wife was attacked. I'm so sorry son, Sara has passed."

Arthur was trying to make sense of what he was hearing. This couldn't be real. He took a step forward. He tried to keep his balance, but the news was too much for him. The earth was moving under his feet. Everything to him became blurry. "Sara...Oh God No!" He began to cry. The two men had to catch him before he fell. He dropped his helmet onto the ground. It made a loud thump sound that seemed to echo in the stillness of Arthur's now empty world.

"NO!" he shouted. It was the cry of someone suffering total agony. Someone who had just had everything in the world taken away from him in an instant.

August 15, 2018

Marine Corps Base Camp Pendleton 11:50 AM

The hall of the military building was quiet, but suddenly filled with the sound of boots. Two MPs were walking towards the mess hall. Major Murphy accompanied them. Major Murphy was a man in his early thirties with blue eyes and blond hair. He was a handsome man but with a little ruggedness to his looks. He held a cold expression on his face. Under his arm, he held a folder. In the hall, the three men stopped and saluted a Lieutenant Colonel who saluted back. The three men continued walking towards the mess hall.

They stepped inside. There was a loud roar of voices from soldiers having lunch. As the Marines inside saw the three men enter the room, the roar was brought to a silence as everyone stood up at attention. Two soldiers were talking at a back table and didn't notice the three men approaching at first. One soldier was bragging about a girl at a bar who was well endowed in her chest. He was in his early 20's and had sandy blond hair cut to a buzz. His eyes were brown and he had a tough quality about him that made him seem a little self-absorbed. The other soldier was laughing as he took a bite of his meal. He was a redhead with freckles that covered his face. He was also in his early 20's. He was sort of a follower to his friend, always believing everything that came out of his buddy's mouth. When they both noticed the men walking towards them, they looked up at each other, and stood at attention. What one MP said to the two men shocked the entire room.

"First Lieutenant John Quinn and First Lieutenant Tim Stevens, you are both under arrest. Please put your arms behind your backs." Quinn and Stevens looked at each other and Quinn spoke up.

"What's this all about?" The MPs didn't answer them. They instead pulled the two Marines' arms behind their backs and began to handcuff them. Quinn looked up at Major Murphy and said angrily; "Sir, there must be some mistake. We didn't do anything Sir. Is this a joke?" The MPs didn't answer them. Quinn looked up at Major Murphy. "This must be a mix-up. We didn't do anything Sir. What's going on?" Major Murphy opened up the folder he had been carrying under his arm. He then looked at the two Marines being arrested.

As they were having their rights read to them, Major Murphy finally spoke up.

"Just cooperate, gentlemen. These are serious charges against the two of you. It's best that you do."

Stevens spoke up. "What charges, Sir?"

After a long pause, Major Murphy sighed, and then spoke up.

"You two Marines are both being charged with Murder"

1:05 P.M.

Second Lieutenant Josh O'Riley had been working out hard on the rowing machine at the gym on base.

He was 25, with blond hair cut very high and tight. He was rather skinny, but had muscle tone. Josh was a well-behaved young man, who never caused any trouble in school while growing up. His grades were always important to him and he did his best to keep his grades up. He came from a loving family in Tennessee, where he had regularly helped out on his dad's farm. He wanted to go to college and although his parents were supportive, he knew they couldn't afford to send him, plus it was hard for him to balance work and school at that time. The military was a good way to not only get free school, but also to pursue his dream of becoming a pilot. He joined the Marines as soon as he graduated high school and turned 18. When he had finished basic training, he started his college courses soon after. He did well in his classes and after completing college and flight training, he finally had the career he dreamed of. He enjoyed being a pilot. Being up in the air felt magical to him. He couldn't imagine doing anything else.

After 45 minutes, Josh finished his work out and walked into the dressing room. He went over to his locker, got undressed and went to the shower. The cool water felt good on his hot skin. He just stood there for a few minutes letting the water cool him off. He missed home. He knew what he was doing was important, but he hadn't seen his parents in over a year and it was taking a toll on his morale.

He finished up cleaning himself and turned off the water. He wrapped a towel around his waist and headed back to his locker and started getting dressed. He glanced over at the picture hanging on his locker door. It was of him and Ann, a pretty girl he had been dating for a couple of years. Josh pulled out a ring from his pocket and held it in his fingers. He didn't want to wait any longer and was planning on proposing to Ann tomorrow on their date at the movies. Josh put the ring back in his pocket and finished getting dressed.

As he was just putting on his shirt and about to head out of the locker room, he heard footsteps behind him. When he turned to see who it was, he was face to face with two MP's. He didn't have a clue what was going on. He looked over and saw Major Murphy standing by. Before Josh could speak, one of the MP's said "Second Lieutenant Josh O'Riley?" Confused, he verified that it was him. "Put your hands behind your back, Son." Josh's mouth dropped. He looked at his commanding officer.

"Sir, what's going on?" Josh put his hands behind his back as instructed and let the two MP's put on the cuffs. He was scared, but didn't want to cause any trouble for himself. Major Murphy spoke up.

"Second Lieutenant Josh O'Riley, you are being charged with the murder of Mrs. Sara Blake. Just cooperate and this will be easier on you, son." Josh was in shock at his words.

"What? I don't understand." He couldn't believe what he just heard. He put his head up against the locker as they were reading him his rights. Josh tried to keep his composure. He was confused. He felt that it was all a joke, but the expression on the three men's faces showed otherwise. He spoke up with barely a whisper. "Wait! What? Sara? Oh God! Sara's…. dead?"

2:12 P.M.

Major Murphy sat in a chair across from Lieutenant Colonel Brown. The Lieutenant Colonel was in his mid-thirties with thinning brown hair. He wore glasses and his receding hairline made him look older than he was. Lieutenant Colonel Brown was sitting at his desk looking over the three files of the arrested pilots. The Lieutenant Colonel spoke up

"I don't believe that these boys would do something like this. There must be a mistake, I mean, murder? These boys seem incapable of all this kind of thing. Their records are squeaky clean."

Major Murphy interrupted. "Well, they were the only ones in the house that evening, other than Corporal Amanda Bishop, who found Mrs. Blake deceased the next morning. So, we have a dead wife of one of our pilots, and those three other pilots are being charged with her murder. I don't know who did what, but none of them are admitting anything, or they are protecting each other." Lieutenant Colonel Brown scratched his head and rubbed his eyes.

"I just can't believe all this. There just has to be a mistake."

"No mistake about it, she is dead and those three Marines are the only ones who were unaccounted for at the party." Major Murphy sat back in his chair and let out a sigh. After a moment of silence between them,

Lieutenant Colonel Brown asked, "So how is Major Blake taking all this?"

"He's taking it as can be expected." Major Murphy said. "He was shipped back home immediately when he was informed. He's on convalescent leave and I believe he's being kept in the infirmary due to a possible suicide attempt."

"Oh God!"

"Yeah, he apparently tried to take some pills. I've been informed he is being given something to help him sleep. She was the world to him. I guess it was just too much to take. I can't imagine what I would do if I were going through what he is. They'd have to keep me sedated, that's for sure." The Lieutenant Colonel rubbed his forehead.

"I don't get any of this. Something just isn't right! Not right at all."

Chapter Two

August 16, 2018

5:30 PM

Ann couldn't believe that she was being stood up. Josh was late and she thought that he better have a damn good excuse for not showing up. She looked at her watch as she stood with her back to the side door of the theater. She saw a young couple walk by and the girl smiled at Ann. She gave a weak smile back and looked again at her watch. Twenty-five minutes late. The movie was about to start. It was one she had wanted to see for quite some time. "He had better have one damn good excuse!" she said under her breath. She had put on makeup and had her hair done to look nice for him, which had turned out to be a waste of her time, she thought to herself. She watched as people stood in line to buy their movie tickets. Some small kid was jumping up and down with excitement.

"Can we go in yet, Mom?"

"We have to buy the tickets first, honey." the mother replied.

"But we'll miss it, I just know it." The little boy was getting even more impatient. The movie had already started by now. Ann wondered if she should just go buy her ticket and go inside by herself and watch the movie, or give him a few more minutes. There was no point in waiting; he wasn't going to show up. Since he had been preparing for a six-month tour in Japan, he was working more hours, but she knew that wasn't it. He hadn't called her the night before. He was afraid of commitment. She knew that was the reason. He seemed nervous when the topic of marriage was ever brought up by her. Most men are afraid of confronting that subject. Josh was one of them. Ann pulled out her cell phone, called his number but no answer. She put her phone away and looked over at a newspaper stand nearby. She stopped cold as she glanced at the cover page. She read the headline:

THREE LOCAL MARINES ARRESTED FOR MURDER. She moved over to the stand to read the article.

She read on: *Sara Blake, wife of Captain Arthur Blake of squadron 446 at Beaufort Marine Corps Air Station was found dead 2 days ago.*

Ann gasped. Sara was one of the wives she was friends with from the squadron. How can this be real? Ann read on. *It appears she was also sexually assaulted. The cause of death hasn't yet been determined. An autopsy is scheduled to be performed. The three local Marines arrested were identified as First Lieutenant J. Quinn, First Lieutenant T. Stevens and Second Lieutenant J. O'Riley of Squadron 446.*

Ann's heart fell. Josh? She could barely keep reading, but had to make sure she read it right.

The article went on to read: *Captain Arthur Blake was immediately notified and flown in from Japan where he was advanced party for the squadron's six-month tour of Japan. No other information is known yet.*

She couldn't believe her eyes. Josh? Murder? She just couldn't believe it! No! This is wrong!

"Oh God!" she gasped. Ann almost fell over. She knew there was a party a few days ago. Josh had invited her, but she had to work and couldn't make it. He called her later that evening, after the party. Nothing out of the ordinary was discussed. He invited her to see the movie tonight.   Murder, possible rape? Oh God! No wonder Josh never called her last night and hadn't arrived for their date.   He had been arrested.

Ann ran from the theater to her car, and drove straight to her mother's house.

JAG Officer Karen Stewart hadn't slept much the night before and was trying to stay awake as she shifted through her pile of paperwork.   She was receiving several calls from the mother of Private George Hill. She needed reassurance that he wasn't going to get discharged for a prank of vandalism to the fountain out by the front gate of the base. He had added dish detergent after his buddies at the barracks dared him to.

Karen was tired of these petty court-martial cases. She was in a rut and wanted something more exciting than representing Marines charged with vandalism or domestic disputes. She was filling up another cup of coffee when her daughter rushed in the house. Karen almost dropped the coffee cup as Ann entered the kitchen. As she looked at her daughter, she could see terror in her eyes. Karen was about to ask her daughter what was wrong but the words didn't make it out of her mouth in time.

"Mom, I need your help! Josh was arrested!" Ann opened up her tablet that was on the counter. She showed her mother the news article. Karen picked it up and began to read it aloud. She walked across the room as she read.

"Sara Blake is dead, and Josh is being charged with it? "Josh? This can't be right. Rape and Murder?" Ann grabbed the tablet.

"Mom, Josh didn't do this! We have to help him!"

Karen sighed.

"Sweetheart, how do you need my help?"

Ann looked at her mother with a serious expression.

"I want you to defend him, Mom. I want you and Mike to prove he didn't do it."

Karen saw the desperation in her daughter's eyes. She had wanted something new and less mundane for a case and with rape and murder; it doesn't get much less mundane than that. Karen took a drink from her coffee mug and leaned against the counter behind her.

Ann's eyes never left her mother. Ann loved Josh. She didn't want him to be in the brig. He didn't belong there with real criminals. If he was convicted of rape and murder, he could get life or even worse, the death penalty. Tears filled her eyes as she thought of that. "Mom, please! I don't want him to spend the rest of his life in prison or worse." She began to sob.

Karen looked up from her cup and over at her daughter.

"Ann, you know him better than anyone. If you are certain he is incapable of this crime, then I believe you." She put her arm around her daughter. "Ann, think hard and be honest with me. Has Josh acted weird lately, shown an aggressive side to you? I need to know."

Ann looked her mother in the eyes.

"Never! Mom, I know he didn't do it!" Ann's voice began to crack as tears ran down her face. "Please Mom! Help him!"

Chapter Three

Arthur lay in his hospital bed. He was groggy from the sedatives they were giving him. He suddenly remembered where he was and what happened. He looked at the IV tube hooked up to his arm. Had it been a day, a week since he heard about Sara's death? He was unaware of what day it was. He had been kept from his cell phone, newspapers, TV and radio. He was glad that they kept him sedated. He didn't want to be alive without Sara.

He looked at the wall across the room, then down to his hand. A tear ran down his cheek as he stared at his wedding ring. He spun it around his finger. He had a window in his room that looked out to a park across from the hospital on base. It was open and he could hear laughter from children in the distance. He wanted to get up and close the window and block out the sound, but he didn't want to see out. He might see a couple holding hands or a happy family with kids and he couldn't stand the thought of that. He felt like he had no soul. He felt like just a body. He wondered how his heart could still be beating, how his breath was still coming, and how he was still alive in this world without her. He couldn't believe that the instant that she died, that he didn't fall over dead himself. He was mad. Mad at the world for still existing, mad at himself for going away and leaving her, mad at his buddies for not protecting her and he was mad at God for taking her while still keeping him alive to live in a world of constant sorrow and loneliness.

They were planning on starting a family when he was to get back from his six-month deployment to Japan. He tried not to think about that. Thinking was too painful. He turned his head as the door to his hospital room opened. A nurse came in. She gave a smile.

"Time for your medication, Captain Blake." She lifted up his arm and gave him a shot. It hurt but he didn't flinch.   He wouldn't allow himself to feel anything. There was no point in it. "It's a beautiful day out today. Maybe we can get you some fresh air later." Arthur, without looking at her, spoke up. "There is nothing beautiful now."

She gave him a sad look. She left after fluffing up his pillow and taking out his lunch tray that he didn't even touch. He had refused to eat and his belly was rumbling for food but he wouldn't allow himself to think about food. There was no point. He wanted to starve.

Outside his room, he heard men's voices. He recognized one to be that of his commanding officer, Major Murphy. The other voice was his doctor's. He tried to listen to what they were saying. It was muffled, but he could make out some of it.

"How is he doing today, Doctor?" Major Murphy asked.

"The same, Sir. He just keeps staring at the ring on his finger, spinning it around. He won't eat, won't talk or show any emotions. He's just blocking out the world around him."

"I can't blame him for that. It has to be the worst thing to go through, especially since he wasn't here to protect her, he must feel somehow to blame."

"People usually do when they aren't around when loved ones pass tragically like this. It's the saddest thing to see. I'm worried about his health though. If he doesn't eat soon, we'll have to feed him through an IV.

Arthur felt the medicine kick in and he drifted off to sleep as he heard the rest of the conversation about him.

"We'll do what we can, Sir; but if he doesn't cooperate with us soon, we'll have to transfer him to the psychiatric ward. I would hate to do that to this young man."

"I know, and I would hate to lose such a good man." He's one hell of a pilot, and soldier. I can't imagine how he'll take it once he hears that his friends are responsible for his wife's death."

Josh was thinking of writing a letter to Arthur. He wanted his best friend to know that he didn't kill his wife, that he didn't have anything to do with the rape and murder. The whole ordeal was hard on Josh too. He was very fond of Sara. He remembered that night at the party. She was so upset that Arthur had left for Japan for six months and she was lonely. He felt sorry for her. Now he was mourning her, and on top of that, he was in the brig on charges of her rape and murder.

As he was remembering that night, an MP interrupted him.

"Second Lieutenant Josh O'Riley, you have a visitor."

Josh was surprised and relieved to see Ann sitting behind the glass of the visitation room.

"Ann!" His face lit up when he saw her. She smiled back at him. He wanted to embrace her but it was impossible with the glass separating them. He sat down quickly and picked up the phone. She did the same on her side of the glass. He spoke up first.

"How have you been?"

"Fine, I guess. How are they treating you here?"

"Well, not much different than the barracks really." he said with a little smile. "They wake me up early; feed me three squares a day. My roommate snores. So, it's pretty much the same." He smiled. He was trying to make her smile. It worked a little. For a moment, they sat in silence.

"Ann, do you think I did it?" He looked very serious as he asked her. He wanted to know the truth about her feelings for him.

"No! I know you didn't do this. I'm so sure that I'd bet my life on it."

He was relieved. He smiled sweetly at her.

"Thank you for believing in me."

"I was mad at you when you didn't call me or show up for our date. I just thought you were afraid."

"Afraid of what?" He sat closer to the glass.

"You know, of commitment. Since things are more complicated..." He interrupted her. "I would never run away from you. You know that! I just was too busy getting arrested." A tiny smile showed up on her lips. He was always making jokes to cheer her up when she was upset.

"I know that now, Josh; and I also know that you couldn't have done it. I know that you could never do anything to hurt another person, especially Sara. That's why I love you so much."

"I love you too, baby." He put his hand up to the glass and she put her's up as if to touch him through the glass. He wanted so much to break through that glass and hold her. He wanted her to know that he was always going to be there for her; even if he couldn't hold her.

"Did you talk to your mother?" he finally asked her after a moment of silence.

"Yes."

"Well, what did she say? Is she going to represent me?" He held his breath. He really wanted Ann's mother to be his attorney in this case. Even though she didn't seem to think much of him dating her daughter, he knew she was one of the best JAG attorneys in Southern California.

"She said yes." O'Riley let out a sigh.

"Great!"

"I wish I could make her see how much of a great guy are and that dating a Marine isn't a bad thing."

Josh looked up at her with a puzzled expression on his face.

"Does she think I did it?"

For a moment, Ann remained silent, looking at the MP behind Josh. He was a skinny man in his fifties. Could he really stop Josh if he punched him out and broke through the glass to be with her? She thought to herself. Finally, she looked back at Josh.

"It doesn't matter what she thinks, she agreed to represent you. That's all that matters. She's the best and she'll get you out of this mess."

"But it does matter, Ann! Especially now! You know that!"

Ann looked down. She didn't want him to bring up the reason she really thought he was running from commitment. Just as if Josh could read her mind, he asked her, "Did you tell her about the…." Ann interrupted him. "Not yet! I need a little time. I don't know exactly how to tell her."

Josh leaned back in his chair. He licked his lips and let out a sigh. "She's gonna find out, and that's why I need to know if she thinks I did it. We're gonna need her support!"

Ann sensed his seriousness. It touched her that he really cared what her mom thought about him.

"She isn't sure yet, Josh. I think it's all just a shock to her. She needs more time to think about it, to get to know you better before she sees how amazing you are."

Josh leaned back and put his hand up to his eye. He wiped away a tear. "Tell her that she's got plenty of time to get to know me. I've got nowhere else to be for a while."

Chapter Four

Karen quickly ate up the last bite of her sandwich just in time to see CID Agent Mike Walker enter the café. He was a close friend and colleague of hers. They had known each other since they were in college as young Marines. She had been married to his best friend, Jake. Mike was a handsome man with a smile that made her blush. Immediately he spotted her as he walked in and went over to her table to join her.

"You're late!" she said as she wiped her mouth with a napkin.

Mike smiled at her and apologized. She quickly forgave him as soon as he gave her that beautiful smile, the one that turned her into butter. He sat down next to her and opened up a briefcase he had been carrying.

"I got caught up at the office, sorry. I got away as soon as I could. I guess you started without me." He pointed to the empty wrapper on the table in front of her.

"Yep. I was starving. Court can go on forever. So, tell me what you know."

"What, no hug first?" he asked with that smile of his. "I haven't seen you in months!"

She looked up at him and smiled. "You help me win this case, and I'll think about it, but for now, tell me what you know."

The waitress came by and asked Mike what he would like.

"Coffee, black, please, and a piece of your delicious looking peach pie, to go." The waitress smiled.

"Sure, I'll be right back."

After the waitress walked away, Karen asked him to tell her what he knows so far on the Sara Blake case. He pulled a file from his briefcase and put it on the table. He leaned in and said "OK, supposedly, this is how it goes. August 14th, there's a squadron party at the home of Amanda Bishop, a Corporal from the squadron. It's your average get drunk and stupid Marine party. Everything seems fine until the next morning when she goes to clean up and discovers the deceased body of Sara Blake in the upstairs guest room. Sara is the wife of Arthur Blake, a pilot from that same squadron." Karen interrupted. "I know Sara. She's an acquaintance of Ann. Was," she corrected. Mike continued. "Sorry, I had forgotten. Okay, Blake was in Japan at the time. He was part of advance party, so he took his flight earlier than the rest of the guys from the squadron. Anyway, Amanda called the police once she realized that Sara was dead. We just found out that Sara had been sexually assaulted that night."

Amanda told the officers what she knew; that three of the Marines at the party disappeared in the house for about ten minutes. Amanda said she went inside soon after to use her upstairs bathroom. She said she remembers she heard First Lieutenants Quinn and Stevens leaving the upstairs guest room as she was using the facilities up there. She said they were both talking about something they had done and to keep it a secret. She said she is certain it was their voices. Second Lieutenant O'Riley was in the house for about five minutes previously taking Sara to the guest room to lay down. She had not been feeling well. He helped her to the bedroom, then he used the bathroom downstairs. She said she doesn't know what O'Riley actually did while in the house with Sara. We do know his dog tags were found in Sara's hand. Bad move on his part. So, they made the arrests. It had to be one or even all three. That is all we know."

The waitress arrived with his pie and coffee. Mike thanked her and began to add sweetener to his drink. Karen spoke up.

"So, the three of them, probably drunk and feeling a little adventurous, took Sara upstairs, maybe she knew what was about to happen, maybe not. Maybe she was in on it at first. Or maybe three soldiers took advantage of a Marine wife separated from her husband away overseas. Maybe as she was struggling and screaming for them to stop, one of them tried to keep her quiet and took it too far? Maybe smothered her, and the other two are covering for their buddy."

"It seems that way. But Karen, you of all people should know that not everything is what it seems with murder cases where more than one person is a suspect."

She finished the drink of coffee she had taken. "I know! But is there something specific we need to focus on here?"

"Well, we just need to keep an open mind about things. So far, the sexual assault was apparent. She had tears around her vagina. Not even the most serious masochists would want to go through that. It appears her death was from asphyxiation. Probably while the rape was going on. But we have to wait until the autopsy is performed. Everyone at the party has been questioned." He handed her some papers. "Here are the names and statements. Amanda was brought in for questioning but isn't a suspect at this time. Their phone numbers are on there as well. Keep your ears open when you question everyone. Something unexpected may show up." He stood to go.

"Don't I always?"

He smiled that smile again and spoke. "Dinner, my place Tuesday? We can go over any new information you may get. I'll make Italian."

"You're on!" she answered. He was getting to her. She couldn't help it. They had been friends for a while and she tried to keep it on a professional level but she didn't know if she could. He made her feel like a high school girl crushing on the captain of the football team each time he smiled at her. But he was just a friend, she kept telling herself. Her late husband Jake's best friend.

Karen put her purse on her kitchen counter. The piece of paper that Mike had given her, she put next to the phone. She checked her answering machine when she saw the blinking red light. It Was Brenda, George's mom. George was Karen's client, the one who put soap in the water fountain. Brenda was calling her nonstop, it seemed. "I just wanted to make sure that you were still representing him and that you will show up at his court-martial next week. I'll call later, Bye!" She rolled her eyes. This poor lady would not leave her alone. Karen hoped she wouldn't show up at her house. She erased the message from Brenda and picked up the page with the name and numbers Mike had given her earlier.

"Well, I guess I better get started." she said to herself. She dialed the first number on the list. Amanda Bishop; The lady who found the body of Sara. It rang twice before Amanda answered. "Hello?"

"Yes, Hello, Amanda Bishop?"

"Yes, this is she."

"Amanda, this is JAG Officer Karen Stewart. I'm representing Josh O'Riley. Officer Mike Walker told you I was going to call?"

A moment of silence

"Oh, yes. I remember. You want to question me too, huh? I already told the officers everything I can remember."

"I'm sure you did, Miss Bishop, but I also need to get all the facts too, just in case they missed something. Now how about meeting at Oscar's Café, say 4:00pm?"

Another moment of silence.

"Okay that's fine."

"Great! See you then." Karen hung up. She didn't know why, but she didn't think that Amanda was going to be easy to get information from. She walked to her desk and began to read the statement from Amanda. She needed to figure out what to ask Amanda to possibly get more information. Karen was good at that. She knew that there was always more than what witnesses could initially remember if she asked enough questions in the right way.

Karen walked to the refrigerator for a drink. It was hot outside and she needed some bottled water to refresh her. When she opened it, she noticed that the 4 pieces of leftover pizza were gone. Knowing that Ann ate like a bird made Karen confused. "Oh, well." she thought. Ann must have had a friend over for lunch or something.

Amanda sat smoking her third cigarette since she arrived at the café. For a Marine, she was actually quite feminine looking. She had beautiful red hair she had pinned up in a bun. She was dressed in her camo. She just came from work at the hanger. Amanda was a plane captain. She was responsible for doing examination and maintenance on the jets in her squadron. She was close with all the pilots.

Amanda didn't want to be bothered with questions again, but she didn't like the idea of her buddies being in the brig. Karen was five minutes late and Amanda thought about just getting up and leaving. Just as the thought occurred to her, she noticed a woman approaching her table.

"Corporal Amanda Bishop?"

She nodded as she blew out a puff of smoke.

"Hi, I'm JAG Officer Karen Stewart. Nice to meet you." Karen extended her hand to shake Amanda's. Amanda reached out her hand and extinguished her cigarette with the other. They shook.

"I'm sorry I'm running a few minutes behind today. I would have texted you if I had a second."

Karen took the seat across from Amanda.

Amanda spoke up. "Oh, I hate text messaging. You never know who you're really talking to. It's so impersonal. I just had a piece of pie. Would you care for anything?"

"Sure, I'll have the same and a diet cola."

Amanda gave her a funny look.

Amanda smiled, looked back at her. "Pie and diet cola. I know, it defeats the purpose."

Amanda waved her hand in the air.

"Hey Ethel, bring out another round of pie and a diet cola, would ya?" The lady behind the counter whom Amanda was speaking to answered. "Sure thing, Amanda."

Karen looked surprised. Clearly Amanda had been in here before, she thought. Just like Amanda had read her mind, she said, "I come in here all the time for pie. I'm sure gonna miss this place while I'm gone. We're going to Japan in two weeks. I get a little nervous before big deployments. I also go through cigarettes like mad."

"Wow, it must be a stressful thing, going on a long trip like that."

"It sure is! It takes like two days to get there. And I'll tell ya, it sure ain't a picnic in the park, being packed in a plane with a bunch of burping, gassy guys for so long. Not exactly my dream vacation, if you know what I mean."

Karen laughed. "I guess it wouldn't be when you put it that way."

Ethel walked up with Karen's pie and soda.

"Thank you." Karen said with a smile.

"Sure thing." Ethel smiled back at her and said "Let me know if you need anything else." before she walked away.

"It looks delicious!" Karen said as she looked at the pie in front of her.

"It's just as good as homemade." Amanda said.

Karen took a bite. "Oh, you're right!"

Amanda reached over and took out another cigarette from its box. "I'm not only nervous about the long flight coming up, I'm a little shaky about the whole ordeal."

Karen put her fork down and reached into her purse. She pulled out a micro-cassette player and hit record. "Oh, do you mind?"

Amanda shook her head. "Knock yourself out!"

Karen put the cassette player on the table and hit record. "Are you ready to begin then?"

"Why not."

"Ok, so were you and Sara friends?"

"No, I mean not really."

"Were you enemies, would you say?"

Amanda took another draw from her cigarette and blew.

"We were acquainted. We talked in passing. We didn't hang out or anything. But we always would speak at parties. It was usually the men in their groups and the ladies in theirs. She was a little withdrawn. I think she was really just shy. She didn't really open up much. But she was really nice. I was closer with Blake than with her, but not in the way you think. I mean I saw him just about every day, since we work together." She smiled. "I'm just one of the guys around work. That's how they think of me."

Karen took another bite of pie while Amanda was talking. "I did invite her to my party though, everyone else's wives and girlfriends were going to be there."

Karen took a drink of her soda, then spoke up. "Did you have any ill-feeling towards Sara, any at all?"

Amanda shook her head. "No, but she had some towards me I think."

"Why do you think that?"

"Well, because I think she was jealous of the time that I spent with Blake. He's at work most of the time and she hardly saw him. I'm the only female in the squadron, so I guess it may cause some speculations with a wife or girlfriend. Anyway, I just had a feeling that she felt that way."

"So, you and Arthur never had any romantic feelings for one another?"

Amanda laughed, then said, "Not a chance. You see..." She paused for a moment. "I'm dating an older guy. The guys at work don't know. I don't want anyone knowing about it. It could cause him some trouble if you know what I mean."

"Oh, I see!" Karen answered. She assumed she meant she was dating a married man and so she left it at that.

Amanda smiled.

"Yep, now you get it."

Karen finished the last bite of pie. Just then, Ethel came and took away their plates. When she was gone, Karen bummed a cigarette from Amanda. "You smoke?"

"Only occasionally. Now please tell me all about that day. The day of the party. Please start with all you remember."

Amanda got silent for a moment. She leaned back to get comfortable before starting.

Finally, she spoke up. "Well, early that morning, Blake left for Japan. See, he was advance party for the deployment. That meant he and a few others in the squadron had to be there in Japan earlier than the rest of us to prepare for our arrival. Well, I had planned a shop party. I had actually planned for it to be the night before so all the squadron could be there, but I had a migraine and so I had to move it to the next evening so those of us that were still here could have a party. I hadn't thought about inviting Sara because Blake wasn't there, but Major Murphy, our CO, figured she was probably sitting home alone and so he suggested I call her up and invite her over. She had been to our parties before with Blake and she knew everyone who was going. She didn't want to at first. Blake had just left and she didn't feel much like partying, but I talked her into it. I knew it would be good for her to get out of that house. It took some convincing, but she finally agreed to stop by for a while. The party started at 5pm that evening, August 13th. She was one of the first to show up. Pretty soon the place was packed."

"Who was there?"

"Everyone in the squadron who wasn't advance party, plus some wives and girlfriends."

"And how many people would that be?"

Amanda thought for a moment. "About 20, including myself."

"Tell me about how the evening went. Who did what, that sort of thing."

"Well, everyone began to drink right off the bat. I had rented a keg. They hit that pretty hard. Then Major Murphy started the bar-b-q. Everyone had brought what they wanted to cook.

It was pretty much help yourself to the grill. Most of the guys were standing around talking about the upcoming deployment, others were playing horseshoes in the yard. We were all in the backyard. I kept the house locked. I wanted to contain the mess outside. My neighbor, who was also at the party, let the guests use his bathroom. I don't want those guys using mine. Some of those guys can get pretty messy. I've had so many parties that these guys know the drill. Anyway, me, Sara and a few of the wives and girlfriends sat on the porch around the table and talked."

"How did Sara act?"

"Pretty bummed. I tried to cheer her up some. I made jokes, and she loosened up a little. Not much, though. They hadn't been married very long and it was his first big deployment since they got married. It was hard on her. She doesn't have any family around here. They're all in Florida." Amanda stopped to get a drink.

"Did anyone act strange, out of the ordinary around Sara that night?"

"They all were drinking, but nothing in particular that I can remember. Sara really just sat with me on the porch drinking her wine cooler while the guys were in huddles talking sports, girls, that sort of thing. Up until she said she felt a little woozy. I told her I'd take her to go lay down upstairs in the guest bedroom until she felt well enough to drive home. I keep a combination lock on the side garage door. I was about to get up and go unlock it and help her in but O'Riley came over and helped."

"She started feeling woozy? "Karen interrupted.

"Yeah, said she must have had too much to drink. I thought that was a little odd, since she only had one or two wine coolers. It takes me at least four or so beers before I start feeling anything. I guess I have a strong system. But she is also a bit skinnier."

Karen lifted up her glass to Ethel for a refill. "Please, go on."

"Well, I remember O'Riley was at the grill at that time. He had just put his steak on. He asked Major Murphy to take over for him on the grill and then he came over. He saw me get up to help Sara, who was kind of wobbly. He said he would help her inside. I whispered the lock combination to him and asked him to just leave it unlocked since I was going to need to use the restroom very soon. So, then he took her around the corner of the house to go unlock the garage door and take her inside. Well soon after he took her inside, maybe about 2 minutes later, I noticed Quinn and Stevens headed around the side of the house where the garage door was unlocked. At that point I thought screw it! I guess I'm cleaning bathrooms tonight! About 2 ½ minutes later, Major Murphy took O'Riley's steak off the grill, so I went in to tell him his steak was done."

How did you know about how long it had been? Did you look at your watch?"

Amanda smiled. "No. I know it was five minutes because O'Riley had just put his steak down on the grill before he went to help Sara inside and I saw that Major Murphy was flipping it when Quinn and

Stevens went in. You see, O'Riley always cooks his steaks for 2 1/2 minutes on each side. He likes it that way every time he cooks a steak. A minute more and he says it's ruined. But in my opinion, that's way too done for my taste. He asked Major Murphy to take over the steak for him, since he knew exactly how O'Riley liked it cooked and I noticed Major Murphy used his watch to time the steak. I was facing the direction of the grill and the back side of the garage from where I was sitting. Well, I then noticed Officer Murphy was flipping the steak on the grill just as I saw Stevens and Quinn go around the side of the house. I heard the side garage door open."

Karen interrupted. So O'Riley had been gone 2 ½ minutes at the point Quinn and Stevens had gone it?"

"Yes. Then, when I saw Major Murphy take off O'Riley's steak, I knew it had been 5 minutes total since O'Riley had gone in and I noticed I hadn't seen any of them come out yet. So, I decided I would go in and let O'Riley know about his steak, and to gripe at Quinn and Stevens for going inside. They knew I didn't like that." Amanda took a drink, then continued. "The downstairs guest bathroom is at the foot of the stairs. I saw O'Riley coming out of it and told him about his steak being done and asked him if Sara was laying down. He said yes and then he hurried outside. I didn't see Quinn and Stevens anywhere at that point. I figured maybe they were talking to Sara upstairs. I had to go to the bathroom, so I went into the downstairs bathroom. While I was in there, I heard the door to the guest room upstairs open and I heard two sets of footsteps coming down the stairs. Then I heard the voices of Quinn and Stevens."

"How long were you in the bathroom until you heard their voices?" Karen asked.

"It was probably a couple of minutes. I splashed cold water on my face and then I did something kind of funny. I peeked behind the shower curtain. I know it sounds funny, but Quinn and Stevens are known to pull pranks like jumping out from around a corner, making you jump as they snap a picture of it. I get a little paranoid. Luckily neither one was there, so I used the bathroom. Then, after I replaced the toilet paper roll and washed my hands, I searched the medicine cabinet for an aspirin. My head was splitting. So, I grabbed a paper cup, filled it with water and took the aspirin. That's what I was doing when I heard Stevens and Quinn come down the stairs and I heard their voices."

"What did they say?"

"Well, Quinn was the first one I heard. He said, "Now don't breathe a word of what we just did. Protect the brotherhood. Got it?" Then Stevens said, "You think she's okay? Maybe we should go back and check on her." Then Quinn interrupted him saying, "She's just sleeping it off, so just act normal. Got it?" Then Stevens said, "Not a word, brother." Then they were gone. When I finished, I went up and knocked on her door, no answer so I went in and she was mostly covered up by the comforter and sleeping, so I left. To me, nothing seemed wrong. But I couldn't figure out what Quinn and Stevens were talking about. I thought they had gone in and maybe put a fake spider in the bed or some stupid joke like that. So, I dismissed it and went back down to the party."

Amanda stopped to light up another cigarette.

"She didn't look hurt to you? Nothing looked suspicious?"

"Nope, I mean it was getting dark out and I didn't check to see if she was breathing or anything. She just looked like she was sleeping."

"Did you see any dog tags when you were in the room?" Karen asked.

"It was a little dark in the room, only the light from the hallway was lighting up the room. I didn't see dog tags because she was covered up."

Karen was taking notes. "What did you do next?"

"Well, I decided she wasn't going to be driving home so I closed the door to let her sleep it off for the night. I made sure no one was in the house, then I went outside and put the lock back on the door. Then I went to go get a bite to eat and chat with some of the guys. The party went on til 11pm. Since we're on base, they are strict about noise levels late at night. O'Riley was the first to leave, then probably about 10 minutes later Stevens and Quinn left. Soon it thinned out and everyone left, except me and Sara."

"Did anyone leave the party for anything and come back that evening before it was over?"

Major Murphy went for beer about 9:30. He came back with a couple of six-packs about 15 minutes later. But no one snuck off by himself at that point that I noticed."

"So, after the party was over, what did you do?"

"Well, I started to clean up some, but decided it could wait til tomorrow. I was tired and still had a headache from drinking a little bit more than I should. So, I went upstairs to bed."

"Did you check up on Sara again that night before you went to bed?"

"No, as far as I knew, she was sleeping. So, I let her sleep."

"Tell me about the next morning. What time you woke up and what you did right after."

"It was about 8:20am when I woke up. I got dressed, started coffee and made some toast for Sara. Then I went to wake her up, but she wouldn't wake up. I lifted up the covers to see if she was moving, and that's when I saw that she wasn't okay. I came around to the other side of the bed to grab a mirror off the dresser. I wanted to see if she was breathing. I saw it in a movie once. Ya know, check to see if there is any fog? Well, no fog. I saw she wasn't breathing. That's when I looked down and saw something shiny. I looked closer and saw a pair of dog tags in her right hand. I knew better than to touch them. I was freaked out and wanted to call the police, so I ran to the phone in my bedroom and called 911." Amanda blew out smoke from her cigarette. "I was out cold all night. Too much beer. Just like I told the CID and the MP's, I didn't hear any noises that night. That's all I know."

Amanda looked at the watch that was on her wrist. I have to be at work in 20 minutes. Sorry but I need to leave." Karen took her business card and handed it to Amanda. Well, if you remember anything else, anything at all, please call me." Amanda stood to go but Karen put her hand on her shoulder. "Amanda, what do you think happened to Sara?"

Amanda paused for a moment, reached in her pocket and threw money on the table to cover her tab.

"I think there are too many secrets these guys keep in the Corps. They cover each other's asses. They keep quiet about things they shouldn't. It's the pact. To protect the brotherhood."

Chapter Five

Arthur was awake. The drugs they had given him must have worn off. He looked around his room. It was dark. It felt like three o'clock in the morning. He sat up in bed, swung his feet over the edge of the bed and put them on the floor. It was very cold. He stood up and was immediately hit by a head rush. He put his hand against the wall beside him until he was stable. He made his way to the door. He listened for any signs of anyone out in the hall. Nothing. He decided he would take a chance and he slowly opened the door. The hall was empty. To his right, he saw the front desk.

Two nurses were behind the desk; One male and one female. They were making out. "Stop! Not here." the female said.

"Then where?" asked the male.

"Come with me." and she led him away and into a storage room. When the door was shut, Arthur quickly made his way down the hall to the desk. He rummaged through things until he found what he was looking for; The local paper. He was hoping to find out what had happened to Sara and who was to blame. He didn't know who the killer was, but he wanted to kill the bastard. It didn't take long to find the paper, folded up under a file on the desk. He read the headline. It was a couple of days old. It read: *Woman Raped, Murdered. Three Marines Arrested.*

He read the article, skimming through it as fast as he could. When he found out what he wanted to know, he fell backwards into the wall behind the desk. He was in shock at what he had just found out. Not only was she murdered, she was raped and his three best friends were to blame.

He was overcome by emotions. This was the hardest blow he had ever been dealt besides finding out Sara was gone.

Just then, the door to the storage room opened. The two nurses saw Arthur and they rushed to him. "Sir, what are you doing out of your bed this time of night?" the female nurse asked as she was fixing her hair. Arthur didn't speak. She and the male doctor hurried him back to his bed. Once he was lying down, the female nurse said "Time for your pain meds." and the male nurse held him down while she injected him with a needle. Arthur tried to struggle with all his might, which wasn't much at the time, but he was not able to stop her from putting the needle in his arm. "NO!" he yelled at her. He didn't want to go under. He wanted to be awake. He needed to be clear-headed, but the needle went into his arm and she injected a sedative. "Bitch!" he said as he began getting drowsy.

"Yep, she sure can be sometimes." the male nurse said.

Arthur struggled to keep his eyes open, but because they were too heavy, they closed. He opened them, but again they closed. This time, they didn't open. Arthur was out cold.

Josh sat with his trey at a table by himself. He took a bite of his mashed potatoes and pushed his trey away. The food that they served in the brig was even worse than in the chow hall. Josh looked up and saw Quinn and Stevens walking up to him. They put their trays down and sat across from him. "Hey, Josh, how's it going man?" Quinn asked quietly. Josh sighed and spoke up. "I've been better." Stevens looked over at him. "I hear Blake is on Suicide Watch. Man, I can't imagine what he's going through!"

Quinn then spoke up. "They think we had something to do with what happened. Amanda said she heard us talking in the hallway. But we didn't do anything to Sara, I swear!"

Then Stevens added "She was passed out. We know as much as you. We didn't do anything to her."

"Man, your dog tags were found in her room, O'Riley. What do you know that you aren't telling us?"

Quinn added in a whisper, "Man, if something happened between you two in the room before we went in there, you have to say something. Why were your dog tags in there, man? What happened in there?"

Angrily, Josh said in a soft voice, "I must have dropped them or something. Maybe they fell out of my pocket when I helped her onto the bed. But I never did anything other than help her to the room. I left her in there after she laid down. You both know as well as anyone that I didn't do this, or that I have any idea who did! "I'm not a rapist or a murderer! Josh said." I cared about Sara, she was my friend and Blake is my best friend! I'd never do anything to jeopardize that!"

Josh looked Quinn right in the eye. "Man, if you know anything about what happened to Sara, tell me! If you know anything at all, you need to speak up! Don't be protecting anyone! We're facing life!"

Josh knew his buddies for a long time and he knew they weren't the kind of guys who would hurt anyone. Sure, they're a bit immature, pulling pranks, that was it. But he knew they may keep quiet if someone they knew had done something bad who was a friend. At least, they would for a while until their conscience kicked in.

Josh tried to keep his composure, but the whole ordeal was hard for him to handle.

Quinn and Stevens exchanged glances and after a moment, Quinn leaned in towards Josh and quietly spoke up. "Okay, look, there's a chance we know someone who knows more than we do about what happened. But we can't say just yet. If we said who and we're wrong, man, we're totally screwed if we ever get out of here!"

Jose spoke up. "If you know something that can clear us all of any charges and get us out, you have to say something!" He was getting agitated. Why in the world would they keep quiet to protect someone when their freedom and lives were on the line? He didn't belong in the brig and neither did they. He would never have done such a thing to Sara, or to his best friend Blake.

Stevens said after looking around "If she doesn't say anything about it, then we will, I promise!"

Karen sat in her car waiting for the light to turn green. It was hot and she wasn't in much of a mood to be dealing with traffic. She was going to the brig to interview Josh; an event she wasn't looking forward to. She didn't like him much. She wasn't sure why. He did seem like a nice young man, but it was more that he had been taking almost all of her daughter's time. Josh and Ann had been going out a lot. She hardly got to see her daughter anymore. When she did, all she talked about was Josh. It got to the point that the mention of his name would make her want to leave the room.

The light turned green. "Finally!" she said out loud. She pulled up to the building and parked. After going through a metal detector and being frisked by a not-so-friendly female guard, she was led to a room. After a few moments of waiting, a guard brought in Josh, then stood behind him next to the door. Josh smiled when he saw Karen and she nodded at him. "Hi Josh." They shook hands. "Please sit down Josh, and we'll get started. Since I'll be representing you, I will need to know everything you can tell me about what happened."

Josh sat down in the chair across from Karen. He leaned in a little. "How's Ann?"

Karen let out a little sigh. "She's fine."

"Please tell her I miss her, okay? Does she ask about me? What does she say?"

"She talks about you all the time. She's not dealing with this very well, but she thinks you're innocent."

Josh sighed and leaned back in his chair. Then, he looked up at Karen. "And what do you think? Do you think I did it?"

She opened her briefcase and removed her micro-recorder, placed it on the table and hit record.

"Now that's what I would like to find out today. Let's begin, shall we?" she said.

Josh sighed. "Sure."

"Now please, tell me about that night; All you remember."

Josh paused a moment, then began. "Well, I left the barracks around 4:40 that day to go pick something up from the store. Then I arrived at the party around 6pm. I hung out with Major Murphy for a while, talking about the upcoming deployment, then went to play horseshoes with some of my buddies. That's what I did for quite a while. I got hungry and it was finally my turn at the grill so I went to fix myself up a steak."

"What time was that?" Karen interrupted.

"About 7:30pm. That's when I noticed Sara was having trouble walking and I went over to see if she was okay. I asked Major Murphy to take over for me on the grill and then I went to go take Sara inside. Amanda told me the combination to the side garage door. So, I helped Sara in after opening the garage door and I helped her upstairs to the guest room. She laid down. I asked if she was okay. She said yes, that she was just a little dizzy and wanted to rest it off. So, I closed the door and went downstairs to the bathroom. I finished up, washed my hands, and well, I looked into the mirror for a few minutes to practice. You see, I was going to.." He stopped himself before he said anything else. He didn't want to tell Karen that he was about to propose to her daughter.

"You were going to what?" Karen leaned in and asked.

After a long pause, she reminded him that he needed to tell her everything so she could help him. Finally, he spoke up. "I was rehearsing what I was going to say to Ann, because…I was going to propose to her the next day." Karen was not expecting that. She tried her best to keep her composure. He continued on. That's why I went to the store before the party. I was picking up a ring for Ann." Karen took a moment and spoke up. She had to be an attorney now and not Ann's mom. "I see! So, what happened next?"

"I heard a set of footsteps come into the house and go up the stairs, so I finished washing my hands. I couldn't make out any voices because I had the water running. I finished washing up and came out of the bathroom and headed toward the back door. Just then I noticed my dog tags were no longer in my pocket, so I headed back into the bathroom to see if I had dropped them while I was in there. I looked but couldn't find them. I figured they must be outside somewhere. I heard the back door open and someone come in. I opened the door and Amanda was standing there."

"And did she say anything to you?"

"Yeah, she jokingly said Major Murphy was letting my steak burn, I had better stop him. I forgot about my dog tags and I thanked her and went outside to get my steak. I ate, then played horseshoes a little longer with some of the other guys. Then I left."

"What time was that?"

"I think it was about 9:30."

"Where did you go after that?"

"I went to the barracks and called Ann. I asked her to meet me at the movies on the 19th."

"Was anyone at the barracks that night that could confirm that you were there?"

"My roommates showed up about an hour after I did."

"And who are your roommates?"

"Quinn and Stevens."

"Did they act strange when they got there?"

"No. They went to the common area of the barracks to watch tv or play video games for a couple of hours while I just went to bed. They woke me up around midnight when they came back to the room. Pretty soon they were snoring."

Karen asked him if he was sure they were in the barracks when he went to sleep and not gone anywhere.

"I'm sure. They left their wallets and the car keys on a night stand in the room. Plus, there was a Marine on duty all night at the barracks that would know if someone left or came after midnight."

Karen turned off the tape recorder. "Thank you, Josh. I'll let you know if I need anything else from you about your statement."

Karen let the guard know they were done. As the guard came to lead Josh away, he spoke up. "I know you love Ann and want to protect her from bad guys. But I promise you, I didn't do this! I love Ann. She is the world to me and I would never ever do anything to hurt her. Sara was my friend, just my friend, and I didn't hurt her. I didn't do this, I swear!"

Ann pulled into her driveway and parked her car. She knew that as soon as she arrived home, Ann would be waiting, asking her questions about Josh's interview. She was hoping to at least make it in the door before her daughter confronted her, but immediately Ann ran towards her. "Mom, did you see Josh? What did he say? Did he ask about me?"

"Ann, slow down! Let me get in the house first and relax before we talk about Josh." Karen walked to the front door and went inside. Ann trailed close behind her.

"Mom, I'm so worried about him I can't stand it! Please tell me how he looked. Did he look well?"

Karen didn't answer. She put her briefcase on the counter and went to the refrigerator for a soda. She popped the top and took a long drink. It had been a rough day for her and she wanted to unwind a bit before answering her daughter's questions. But Ann wanted to know now! She didn't want to wait for her mother to unwind. She missed Josh and any news from him she wanted to know about right away.

"Please Mom, tell me! How is Josh? Tell me what he said!"

Karen sat down on the couch and sat her soda on the coffee table where she propped up her feet.

She took a long sigh and began. "Yes, I did see Josh. I got his statement. Yes, he did ask about you and he said to tell you that he misses you."

Ann's eyes widened as she smiled. "Thank you!"

Karen gave a half smile as she saw her daughter's reaction.

Karen refrained from mentioning anything about what Josh said about proposing to Ann. It wasn't her place.

Ann's smile faded as a serious expression swept over her face. "Mom, do you believe he didn't do it?"

Karen thought for a moment, then answered. "Sweetheart, you know that I have to do my job whether or not I believe my clients are guilty or innocent. I do my job and defend them at their court-martial. So, what does it matter what I believe as long as I do my job?"

Ann was looking down as she spoke. "Because Mom, I'm pregnant!"

Karen stopped and looked over at her daughter. She was about to say "You're kidding!" but the scared expression on her daughter's face told her otherwise.

Karen's jaw almost hit the floor. She tried to take it all in. She was in shock. Her baby was going to have a baby? She tried to find the right words to say but a soft whisper of, "Oh Ann!" slipped out. Ann looked to her mother for support, for love, for anything other than scolding. A tear ran down Ann's face and her mother did something she wasn't really expecting. She embraced her.

"Oh sweetheart, I understand now why it is so important to you and Josh what I think about all this! I had no idea." Ann softly pulled away from her mother's hug. "Mom, I don't want to have this baby without Josh. We need you to believe that he didn't do those terrible things because we need your support!"

Her mother held her daughter's face in her hands. "Honey, his dog tags were found in her hand, and he was missing for part of that party. If he didn't do it, then he's got to prove he didn't do it. Saying I didn't do it isn't enough. I will do my very best to see that my grandchild is born with their mother and father there to raise them. I just pray that some information that clears him will come up fast!"

Ann let her head fall back on her mother's shoulder. They had five months 'til the baby arrives, but only 1month till the court-martial.

Chapter Six

"Mike, hi! Are we still on for Italian?" Karen had called Mike so they could compare notes.

"Karen! Yes, how about you come over tonight at about 6pm?"

"Sure. I'll see you then."

Two hours later, Karen stood on Mike's porch with her briefcase in one hand and a bottle of wine in the other. She rang the doorbell with a free finger. She thought to herself that maybe she was taking things with Mike too far. After all, it had only been a year since her husband Jake passed away from a car wreck.

Mike opened the door, smiled when he saw her and invited her in.

The house was filled with the wonderful aroma of garlic bread and pasta sauce.

"It smells wonderful!" she said as she stepped inside.

"Thanks! It's just about ready. Please make yourself at home and I'll be back out in just a minute." He went back into the kitchen to finish cooking. She looked around the room. She saw a beautiful dining room set on one side of the room. She walked over to the set table and placed the bottle of wine down on it. Mike had wonderful taste in decorating. Expensive black leather couches on one side of the room, very expensive armoire on the other. A photo in a frame was sitting on the armoire. It was a picture of Karen, Jake and Mike at a lake. She smiled as she picked it up. She remembered that day. They all decided to go hiking. She loved thinking about happy times with Jake, but it was still hard for her. A feeling of guilt ran through her for having dinner with her late husband's best friend.

To take her mind off Jake, she noticed the pricey looking paintings that hung on the walls. She was sure that he hadn't decorated himself. He must have hired a decorator to do it for him. Mike didn't strike her as someone who would take the time to design a room this beautiful. It definitely had a women's touch. As far as she knew, Mike wasn't seeing anyone.

"Hey Mike, did you design this living room yourself?" she asked him as he came back towards the dining room table.

"No, my sister Mindy did. Remember, she's an interior design student now. She used my apartment for practice."

Karen smiled. "Oh, that's right! She did an excellent job."

"Yep, she sure did." He agreed with a smile.

The table was set and dinner was ready. Mike clapped his hands together. "Well, time to eat."

They talked as they ate.   First about how wonderful dinner tasted, then about the weather, about Jake a little, and finally about work.

"I interviewed Josh and Amanda. I transcribed their interviews." Karen opened up her briefcase and handed Mike a pile of papers. Mike finished his bite of bread and reached for the papers. He looked through them for a moment. Mike flipped back and forth from one page of Josh's statement to one of Amanda's. He then spoke up.

Have you interviewed Quinn and Stevens yet?"

She shook her head. "No but they are next on my agenda."

"We'll see if their statements match up with what we have so far. Mike smiled. "Now, would you care for some of my famous cheesecake?"

"Oh absolutely!" Karen said. "By the way, I have some news. Ann is pregnant. About four months along."

"Wow! Are we happy about that considering the situation?" Mike asked as he started clearing dishes.

She looked down for a moment, then spoke. "Honestly, I'm thrilled about having a grandchild! But considering the situation, I'm also very concerned. I mean sure I'll be there for Ann all the way, but I'm not sure if Ann will be okay. She really loves Josh and if he's found guilty."

Mike interrupted. "Hey, you're an amazing mother and just as amazing an attorney." He sat down beside her and put his hand over hers. "Karen, you got this! Together, we're going to find out who did this and clear Josh's name. You have to believe!"

Karen smiled as she looked at Mike. Her heart skipped. He made her feel alive. She hadn't felt that in so long.

Major Murphy knocked on Arthur's door at 9:30 am.

"It's open!" a voice from inside said. Major Murphy entered.

Arthur was lying down looking up at the ceiling. His doctor was with him.

He turned when Major Murphy walked in.

The doctor stood up and greeted Major Murphy at the door. He talked very quietly so Arthur couldn't hear their conversation. "Hello Officer." the doctor said almost in a whisper. "He is doing better. We have lowered his dosage. He's coming around."

Major Murphy gave the doctor a look of confusion and a little anger.

"Are you sure that's such a good idea? I mean he's not quite capable of dealing with this trauma. What if he tries to hurt himself again? It is quite too much for anyone to take. He needs more time."

"Well, he's doing better and we need to get him off the medicine soon so he doesn't become addicted. He's eating now and we wanted that. If we increase his doses, it's just going to hurt him in the long run. He has to face what's happened so he can get through this in his own way. We are watching him at all times. If he tries anything to hurt himself, we will be there to stop him." The doctor stepped back.

Major Murphy took a step forward. He looked at Arthur who looked at him.

"Blake, how are you feeling today?" Arthur licked his lips, looked back at the window and said almost in a whisper, "How do you think?"

The doctor put his hand on the major's shoulder. "Don't push too much, he still is trying to cope."

"I know what I'm doing." Major Murphy said. He turned back to Arthur.

"Son, I know you're angry and..." Arthur turned to look at him quickly.

"You have no idea how I feel sir, I was sent away and my wife was raped and murdered by my friends, and you guys are keeping me drugged so I can't think. Well, I can think now and I want answers."

Major Murphy gave a shocked expression. He wasn't aware that Arthur knew any of the details.

He turned to the nurse next to Arthur's bed. "He was supposed to be kept away from the news!"

The nurse gave a sorry expression. "Sir, he got up a couple of nights ago and found a paper from the front desk when the nurse on duty stepped away for a moment."

Major Murphy shot the nurse a sharp look. "Make sure it doesn't happen again. I don't want him to get a hold of some false information. He needs time to grieve, to process what has happened and how to get back to his life. I need my pilot back in flying condition as soon as possible. He's the best I've got!"

"Sir, we'll make sure it doesn't happen again."

"See that you do!"

Major Murphy walked over to Arthur. "Blake, I'll tell you more when I think you're ready."

Arthur looked at him for a moment. "Sir, how did she die? I need to know."

Major Murphy didn't want to answer that question yet. But he knew Arthur needed to know at least that now.

"They think it was asphyxiation. But an autopsy will tell for sure. We won't know for a while."

Arthur looked down for a moment. "Is it true that Quinn, Stevens and O'Riley were arrested?"

Major Murphy paused. "Yes son, they were the only ones with her in the house that evening."

Arthur stared straight out the window. A single tear made its way down his cheek. How could he lose his wife and be betrayed by his best friends all in the same day? He silently vowed revenge. They would pay! The brig wasn't good enough. He wanted them to feel his pain.

Chapter Seven

K aren sat at the table, her briefcase beside her. She seemed to be waiting forever before Quinn finally showed up. He was led into the room by a guard who closed the door before stepping back against the wall by the door. Karen didn't like being in the room with him even though a guard was very near-by.

She looked over at Quinn. "Second Lieutenant John Quinn, I'm JAG Officer Karen Stewart. She reluctantly reached out her hand. He was a handsome guy, that was for sure. Being handsome and a pilot, he must have several girlfriends, she thought. He smiled at her and looked her up and down. This made her even more nervous and appalled by him. Karen was a beautiful woman. Many times, she was whistled at while walking past a group of soldiers. She was used to being on base around young male Marines. But she didn't want to be looked at like a piece of meat from this creep. He reached over and took her hand. "Well, I can see why O'Riley chose you to represent him. You sure are a pretty looking thing." Karen pulled away and sat down. She fought back the temptation of slapping him and instead, cleared her throat. "As you know I am representing Josh O'Riley. And for the record, I'd appreciate any sexual remarks to be kept to yourself, got it?"

He gave a sly grin. "Yes ma'am, I sure do." Although his expression showed otherwise. "Good!" She continued. "Now if you will sit down, we can get started."

He took his seat but never took his eyes off Karen.

She opened her briefcase and took out her micro-recorder. She pushed the record button and took a deep breath. After a moment, she began.

"Mr. Quinn, please tell me about the night at the party. Tell me all that you remember."

He smiled. "Sure, anything you want, but please call me John."

She kept her straight expression, keeping her eyes on him.

"Well, me and Stevens rode together in my car to the party. We were going to give O'Riley a ride, but he had already left by bus to go stop at a store or something. We're all roommates, ya know."

"Yes, I know."

"Well, anyway, we got there at about 6:50. We really just hung out and played horseshoes and drank beer. We socialized a bit. And that's about all we did."

"Tell me about when you went into the house."

"Well, I heard Amanda ask O'Riley if he would take Sara in so she could lay down. Then I saw O'Riley and Sara going into the house together. He had his arm around her. I thought that was kind of weird. I mean, her husband is away and O'Riley is his best buddy, besides me and Stevens. Well, we went back to talking with a group of buddies we were standing with, but after a couple of minutes, I noticed O'Riley and Sara hadn't come out. We were a little concerned for her. So, me and Stevens decided to go in to see what was going on. When we went inside, O'Riley was in the bathroom downstairs, so we went upstairs to the guest room where Sara was to check on her.

We were a little concerned when we saw she was passed out. We kind of wanted to make sure she was okay, you know, keep an eye on her since Blake was gone. Anyway, she doesn't usually drink much and we assumed she had too much that evening. So, Stevens decided it would be funny to take a picture of her passed out. I agreed."

Karen interrupted. "Why would you do a thing like that? Take a picture of her like that?"

He smiled. "Well, last shop get-together, Blake walked in on me puking my guts out in the bathroom and he took a picture. He showed it to my girlfriend a few days later. Man, I got in trouble for that. My girlfriend doesn't like me drinking at parties when she's not there to keep an eye on me. So, when we saw Sara had passed out while drinking, we got the crazy idea that we would return the prank. Then, when we would get to Japan, we would show the picture to Blake. It was purely innocent, you know. We thought he'd get a little mad, but soon realize we were just innocently getting back at him."

Karen rolled her eyes and gave him a disapproved look.

"Well, anyway, after we took the picture, we heard someone moving around downstairs and decided we would go back down to the party and let her sleep."

He waited for Karen to ask him more questions. She took it all in and thought for a moment.

"Did you notice anything in her hand when you were in there?"

"It was kind of dark. We could see by the hallway light, but we couldn't see her hands. They were under the covers."

Karen was silent. She jotted a few things down on a piece of paper. Then she looked up.

"Is that as it really happened?"

"Yes, Ma'am, it sure is. You can ask Stevens. He'll tell ya."

"So, what did you do next?"

"Well, we came downstairs and went back outside to the party. We stayed till about 9:20pm and headed back to the barracks."

"Was O'Riley there when you got to the barracks?"

"Yes, he was. He was getting ready for bed. But me and Stevens were still wide awake, so we went down to the common area to hang out and watch tv. Some guys were there so we started a game of pool. We did that for a couple of hours, then went back to the room and went to bed."

Karen spoke up. "Did O'Riley stay in his room the rest of the night?"

Quinn smiled. "Yes ma'am. He was asleep until we got back to the room. He was a little angry. We had woken him up but he rolled back over in his cot and went back to sleep."

"Was there anything off about O'Riley that evening either at the party or after at the barracks?"

Quinn thought a moment then spoke up. "He seemed a little withdrawn, like something was on his mind. He wouldn't tell us why he went to the commissary before the party. We asked but he just said he'd tell us soon." We shrugged it off. Didn't think too much about it."

Karen hit the stop button on her recorder and put it in her briefcase.

She stood up. "Okay Mr. Quinn, Thank you for your cooperation. If you remember anything else that could help, please let me know."

"I sure will Karen."

She wanted to correct him and say "Officer Stewart." but she decided he wouldn't care.

She felt like she was going around in circles with all the information she was given. Everyone's story was just a hair off and she wanted to know what the missing puzzle piece that would bring the whole picture together was.

She thought of Mike as she drove home. His dark hair, his blue eyes. She wished he would ask her out on a date and not just to discuss the case. She wanted him to be interested in her on a romantic level as she was of him. She was tempted to give him a call and tell him about Quinn's interview but she shook the idea from her mind. He would ask her to come over. And she was a mess. She longed for a shower. She thought about Ann. She thought about the baby that would come in five months. She didn't want her grandchild to be born without his father. The brig was a terrible place to bring a child to visit his dad. She needed more information. She needed to find the missing piece of the puzzle and try to get Josh off the hook. But where would she find it? She needed to question Stevens. Maybe he had the missing clue.

Arthur didn't take his pill. He hid it under his tongue and spit it out when the nurse wasn't looking. He was tired of living in a cloud. He wanted to be fully aware of what was going on. He walked back to his door. He looked down the hall to make sure no one was coming. He closed the door and walked back to his bed. He lifted up the mattress and took out what he was hiding. The newspaper from the day before.

He had taken it while the nurse went to the bathroom. He had stashed it quickly under his mattress. He had a moment to himself now and he skimmed through the paper looking for some more information on his wife's death.

There it was on page seven. It was a small follow-up article. He read how it said that police are still investigating the crime and how they are awaiting autopsy results. Not much more information. He had a feeling that there was something he knew that would help. Something the police needed to know but he couldn't think. He needed more time to recuperate from the whole trauma. He lay back on his bed and looked out the window. He knew his friends. They were wild at times but he just couldn't imagine them doing anything to Sara. He had flown with them for years and they were like brothers.

Something wasn't right. Someone else had to have done it, not his buddies. He needed to figure out what the truth was and help clear his friends of the charges; if they were in fact innocent. But someone did rape and murder her. Someone from that party. It was only Marines from the squadron that came to those parties.

Marines and sometimes spouses or girlfriends. He didn't want to believe his best buddies would do such a terrible thing. They knew how special Sara was to him; how she was his world. Sara. He couldn't live without her. He wanted to crawl into a corner and die. He wanted to be with her wherever she was to comfort her and tell her that no one was ever going to hurt her again. He would protect her. But she was gone, and he was alive on earth, and as long as he was still alive, he would make sure to find out what happened and make the son of a bitch pay!

Chapter Eight

Karen was feeling the pressure to find out the truth of who killed Sara Blake. She hadn't found out anything that could prove Josh's innocence yet and time was ticking away.

Karen was sleeping when the phone rang at 7:30 am. She was about to yell at whoever it was for waking her up when she heard Mike's voice instead. "Karen, sorry to wake you up but I meant to ask you if you spoke with the husband, Arthur Blake yet?"

She rubbed her eyes. "No. I hadn't really thought about questioning him. He wasn't even there. Why?"

"Well, something tells me that he may help more than we think."

Karen thought for a moment. "Wasn't he questioned already?"

"Yeah, but he's been on pain meds and they couldn't get much from him then."

"I suppose it's worth a try."

I'll call you tomorrow. I'll see if I can set that up. Maybe together, we can find the missing piece." Mike said.

She smiled. She enjoyed working with him as a team.

"Definitely! Give me a time and I'll meet you there."

The next morning Karen jumped in the shower and as she got dressed, she decided to throw on some makeup. She wanted to look nice. Mike was just a friend but she couldn't see the harm in looking desirable to him, making him eat his heart out a little.

She arrived at the cafe at 8:27am. She saw Mike sitting at a table eating a bagel. She noticed how fresh he looked even early as it was. He looked like he stepped out of a modeling shoot. He smiled and waved at her when he saw her walking up. She took the seat opposite of him.

He was still smiling at her when she sat down. She wondered if he would notice her makeup. Her question was answered when he spoke. "Karen, you look nice this morning." She smiled with a slight blush.

"Thanks. You look restful. Did you sleep well last night?" She really wanted to ask if he slept alone last night.

"Yep! I did. Like a baby."

Just then the waitress came over. "What can I get for you ma'am?" she asked Karen.

"I'll have a cup of coffee and a bagel with cream cheese, please."

"Sure, I'll be right back with that."

Karen watched the waitress walk away. Then she turned to Mike.

"So, Mike, you think interviewing the widower who wasn't even in the country will help us find what we are missing?"

Mike finished swallowing down his sip of coffee before he answered.

"Well, I have this feeling that we just need to look everywhere.   Leave no stone unturned. We've questioned almost everyone involved. Arthur Blake may be the one who holds the answer."

"But he wasn't even there. Are you saying that he had someone rape and murder his wife for him while he was gone?"

Mike took another drink of coffee. "No, I'm not saying that, but we do have to keep an open mind and look at the whole picture. Anything is possible, though."

Karen looked down at the table. She became silent. Mike noticed her silence.

"Karen, is there something bothering you? You seem preoccupied with something."

Before Karen could answer, the waitress came over with her coffee and bagel.

"Thanks." she said to the waitress.

When the waitress walked away, Karen spoke up. "It's Ann, I'm just worried about the whole situation of her possibly having her baby without Josh. I'm doing all I can to find out who did this, but I can't move mountains."

"I know this is a tight situation you're in, I can't imagine."

"I try to keep away from a personal level with my clients. I keep it business as much as I can, and try not to get too involved. But as you can tell, this has to be personal now. I have a grandchild on the way in five months. If Josh really is innocent, I only have a few weeks till the court-martial to prove that he didn't do it so my grandchild isn't born with a convicted rapist and murderer for a father."

"What does Ann believe?"

"Oh, she is convinced that he didn't do it. She would bet her life on it. I, on the other hand, just don't know. Who knows what really happened in the time that he went in the house with Sara to the time he came out? Why were his dog tags in Sara's hand? Maybe something did happen."

Mike finished the last sip of coffee. "Maybe Stevens' answers will help in some way."

"Well, if he's anything like his buddy Quinn, I wouldn't hold my breath."

Mike smiled. "You didn't like him much, huh?"

Karen sighed. "Well, he may be one hell of a pilot, but he's also one hell of an arrogant Marine.

When they arrived at the hospital, the headed to the information des.

"May I help you?" the receptionist asked as she looked up at Mike. Karen could tell by the expression on the girl's face that she was blushing at how handsome Mike was.

Karen spoke up. "Yes, I'm JAG Officer Karen Stewart and this my partner. We would like the number to Arthur Blake's room please. We need to ask him a few questions."

"Oh, let me see." the receptionist said as she broke her gaze from Mike down to her computer.

She searched on her computer for a moment.

"Room 103; It's right down the hall and to your left."

"Thanks!" Mike said as Karen pulled on his arm to walk away.

"My pleasure!" the girl said never taking her eyes off   Mike.
As they walked down the hall, Mike smiled. "I think that girl thought I was cute."

Karen rolled her eyes. "Oh, I'm sure of it."

As they came to the window of Arthur's room, Major Murphy, who was standing by the window looked rather annoyed as he saw them approach.

"Who are you?" Major Murphy said.

"I'm CID Agent Walker and this is JAG Officer Stewart. We're here to speak with Arthur Blake about his wife."

Major Murphy got a worried expression on his face. "You guys already asked him questions. He's been through enough already."

Mike spoke up. "Sir, I have not spoken with him. I'm trying to do my job here and I would appreciate your cooperation. We need more information. The nurses have been giving him sedatives and we have to find a window of when he is clear-headed enough to talk to us." Mike looked in the window at Arthur, who was awake and looking back at him. "He looks to be awake now so if you'll excuse us." Mike reached for the doorknob but Major Murphy stopped him.

"You'll have to ask him questions with me in there. I don't want anyone upsetting him more than he already has been!"

"I'm sure you don't, Sir, and we don't intend to upset anyone. But this man's wife has been murdered and a possible innocent man sits in the brig. We need all the facts. But we need you to wait outside in the hall while we speak with him. He is not to be influenced in any way! Now please move!"

Major Murphy became red-faced as Mike and Karen pushed past him and stepped inside and closed the door.

Arthur looked over from his bed at the two people approaching him.

Mike spoke up. "Captain Arthur Blake, I'm CID Agent Mike Walker and this is JAG Officer Karen Stewart. We'd like to speak with you about what happened to Sara.

Arthur looked down. "Someone was here a couple of days ago asking questions. I told them what I know, which is nothing."

Mike spoke up. "Yes, but they only got a minimal amount of information from you because you have been sedated."

Arthur looked confused. "They say I am on suicide watch, that I took some pills. But I don't remember that at all! I'm not someone who thinks like that. That's a coward's way out. Not a Marine!"

Mike spoke up. "I'll see if I can find out more information on why they're keeping you here."

Arthur nodded.

Karen stepped forward. "I'm representing Second Lieutenant Josh O'Riley."

"You're representing Josh?" Arthur asked.

"Yes."

"Well, I hope you can prove him innocent because he's my best friend. I don't believe that he would have done it."

"Can you tell us about Quinn and Stevens?" Mike asked. "Are they capable of a crime like this?"

Arthur thought for a moment and shook his head. "They are a couple of jerks at times, but they are really harmless. It had to have been someone else. But I just can't think of anyone who would have any reason to hurt her."

Mike was writing all this down in a notebook.

Karen questioned him next. "How close were you and Amanda?"

"Amanda?" Arthur was caught by surprise by that question.

"Amanda is my friend at work. She's sort of like a sister to me."

"I need you to be honest here. Were there any feelings romantically between you two?"

Arthur's eyes went wide.

"Absolutely not! She's got some guy she's secretly dating."

Karen gave a small smile.

"Amanda didn't know that I knew, but she's been suspiciously happy lately."

"So, she wouldn't have plotted Sara's murder to get her out of the way to get to you?" Mike asked.

Under any other circumstance, Arthur would have laughed at that question. But he couldn't laugh. He didn't think he ever would be able to laugh again.

"No!" he said as he looked back down to the floor. "I'm sure."

Arthur looked back up after a moment. "Do they still think that she was strangled?" he asked.

Mike looked up from his notepad. "Yes, that's what they think, but until the autopsy results come back, we won't know for sure."

"Was she drugged?"

"Drugged? Mike and Karen looked puzzled. "Not that they can tell. Why?" asked Mike

"It's nothing really."

Mike spoke up. "Arthur, if there is anything you can tell us that would help, please do so; even if it doesn't seem relevant."

Arthur took a deep breath. After a few seconds, he spoke.

"Well, a week before I left for Japan, I spotted one of those old film containers in Steven's locker at the shop while he was in the shower. I hadn't seen one of those since the 90's. It was a little weird since he had a digital camera he used. Well, I thought about how he and Quinn are always taking pictures of people in embarrassing ways so I thought I would pull a prank on them. I would grab the film and get it developed myself and see what pictures they had taken, possibly save someone from embarrassment. Well, when I opened up the container and looked at the contents, I saw that it wasn't film at all. It was little white pills. I looked at them carefully, then I recognized them. I had seen them on TV on one of those evening news programs just a few nights before."

"What was it?" Karen asked.

"It was GHB, ya know, roofies."

Mike looked up. His mouth dropped. "GHB, are you sure?"

"I'm not an expert here but it was the same pills I had seen on the program. I did an internet search on them. Same color, numbers. It was GHB for sure!"

Karen looked at Mike. "What is GHB?"

"It's short for Gamma y-hydroxybutyrate," Mike answered. "Also known as the date rape drug."

Karen looked back at Arthur. "The date rape drug, are you sure that's what you saw?"

"Yes. I'm sure. I confronted him and he confessed. He told me he was not sleeping well at night and having excessive daytime sleepiness and it might help him out, help him sleep. He swore he hadn't taken any yet."

"Did he say where he got it?" Mike asked

"He wouldn't say. He's a lot of things, but a snitch ain't one."

"What did you do?" Karen asked.

"I was concerned. I knew they could be dangerous if he takes them and flies, so I told Major Murphy. He took them away and grounded Stevens from flying for a week. Made him take a drug test, which he passed. I felt really bad about turning him in, but I felt it was the right thing to do. Stevens forgave me. Actually, thanked me for stopping him from making a huge mistake."

"What happened to the drugs?" asked Mike.

"I would assume Major Murphy destroyed them. He was hard on Stevens, but he cares about his pilots. I'm sure he covered for him. Until yesterday, I had completely forgotten about all that. I don't know if that's anything, but I hope that helps somehow."

Karen looked at Mike. They had something. Maybe that was the missing piece.

When they knew that they had all the useful information they could get from Arthur, they thanked him and turned to leave. Arthur spoke up just as they were going out the door.

"My wife was a wonderful woman. She meant everything to me. She was forced into… you know. I know she would never have cheated on me." He began to sob.

Karen went over to his bed and held his hand.

"We're doing everything we can. I promise you; we will continue to do all we can to find who did this to Sara."

Arthur nodded his head.

Mike and Karen walked out of the base hospital. Mike spoke up. "Find out all you can about GHB, and I'll make a call to Bill and give him this new information. If we have what I think we have, this could be the help you need to get O'Riley cleared. You still need to question Stevens." Mike said as he and Karen walked over to the car.

"You suppose maybe too much of the GHB drug could be the killer?" She asked.

"Well, as soon as I give this information to the coroner, he'll check it out for us. But I have a feeling that we already know the answer. Mike opened Karen's car door for her. She turned around and thanked him. She was surprised to see him come closer to her. She thought he was going to kiss her. Her heart skipped. She waited for it. But he quickly pulled away. "My pleasure!" he said. She could tell she was blushing. She was embarrassed. For a moment, she thought he was going to kiss her. She was a little disappointed.

"I miss you!" Ann was trying to hide tears as she sat across Josh who was behind the glass.

"I miss you too, baby." He put his hand up against the glass and she did the same.

"How are you?"

He gave a half smile. "I'm doing okay. I talked some with Quinn and Stevens. They say they don't know anything about what happened to Sara. I don't think that they think I had anything to do with it. They know me and I know them. Someone else did this. The court-martial is in three weeks. I hope something comes up soon."

"Well, Mom will get you out of here. Don't worry. I think she believes you didn't do it. She won't tell me what she knows, but I think that it's going to be over soon."

Josh sat back in his seat. How's the baby doin'?"

Ann put her hand on her stomach. "Fine. I know it's too soon, but sometimes I think I can feel him move."

He moved closer to the glass as if he were going to whisper in her ear.

"When I get out of here, I want us to get married."

She smiled big. "Me too!"

A tear ran down her cheek. She wanted to be his wife. She wanted to live the rest of her life with him and hold him in her arms. She hoped that she would get that chance. The thought of him being locked up forever or even getting the death penalty for a crime he didn't commit frightened her down to her very soul.

He frowned when he saw her tears. "Oh honey, don't cry."

She tried to stay strong.

"Times up." a guard said and helped Ann up on her feet. She looked back at Josh.

"I love you!" he said.

"I love you too!" she sobbed as she was led away from him.

Chapter Nine

Karen sat at her computer. She brought up a web search site. She punched in "GHB" and after a moment, her screen was filled with lists of websites about the drug. She clicked on the first one she saw. It was an article on how it is sometimes prescribed for narcolepsy. It is to help with night time sleep. She thought maybe Stevens' reason was right about why he had them.

She looked and found an article of a fifteen-year-old female who, while on a blind date, had secretly been given the drug by her date and was raped. She was pressing charges.

Karen finished reading that article and clicked on the next one. That article was about how people at raves took GHB for recreation.

Karen clicked on the next article and she found what she had been looking for. A girl was found dead upstairs at a party after her boyfriend slipped the drug GHB in her beer. She had been drinking and the drug's reaction with the alcohol had a deadly effect.

Karen remembered her interview with Amanda. Sara had been drinking but only after just two wine coolers she was feeling woozy and had to go lay down. Maybe it was more than wine cooler in her drinks. Who gave her the drinks? She hadn't thought to ask that question since at the time, there was no reason to.

"Bingo!" Karen said. She switched on her printer and printed out the article to show to Mike.

Mike was on the phone when Karen walked into his office. He waved her in and she sat opposite of him in the chair in front of his desk.

"Okay Bill, just as soon as you can, that would be terrific! Tell Bonnie and the kids I said Hi."

He put the receiver down and looked at Karen. "So, what did you find out?"

She handed him the papers she was holding in her hand. GHB also known as Rohypnol, liquid x, easy lay, fantasy and cherry meth to name a few. It's colorless and odorless, easily hidden in a person's drink. Its effect comes on in fifteen to sixty minutes after ingestion, depending on body size and weight."

Mike interrupted. "Sara was a small girl."

"Yep, but guess what? A girl in Atlanta was found dead upstairs at a party. Police couldn't find out what had killed her at first because it leaves little trace in the body. You have to know to look for it. Her boyfriend finally confessed that he had hidden GHB in her beer in hopes to get lucky. Well, she had been drinking and between the alcohol, the drug and her small size, it had an effect that caused her to go into respiratory distress and she died."

Mike's eyes widened.

"Karen! This has to be the missing piece! Someone must have slipped it in Sara's drink, maybe even accidentally gave her too much and along with the alcohol in her drink, she died. That has to be it!" He looked like he wanted to kiss her. She sure wished he would.

"As soon as Bill gets back to me with the drug test results, we'll know for sure. Karen, this may be just what we were looking for to get Josh free. If it is, he'll be at the hospital, holding your newborn grandchild in five months."

"Hey Mike, you caught me in a bit of a messy situation." Bill, the Medical Examiner said as he had his hand in the torso of a cadaver he was working on. Mike was entering the examining room and tried not to look at the dead body as he kept his distance. Mike had worked with Bill for several years, but was still a bit squeamish when he saw Bill at work.

"Have you gotten any results back on the GHB test on Sara Blake yet?"

"Not yet, still waiting on the Forensic Toxicology team to get back to me. By the way, there seems to be two different types of semen found in her body. Tests are being run right now." Mike was in shock. "Wait, two?"

"That's what it looks like. I'm sorry I can't give you anything more, but it takes time. But I'll let you know the minute I hear back on these test results. I'll call them again in a minute."

They both looked down at the body of the old man who Bill was working on.

"Well, in a little more than a few."

Karen sat in bed going over her notes from interviewing the witnesses so far. She had a couple more to interview. Stevens and Major Murphy. She was feeling tired and needed a break from the case. She thought about calling Mike and asking him to dinner, but she knew it would turn into business. She wanted to go out. She thought about a movie. If they went to see a movie, there wouldn't be time to talk about the case. She looked over at the phone. She then looked at her watch. It read 6:30pm. If she called now, they could make it to a 7:30 show. She picked up the phone and dialed his home number. She held her breath as the phone rang.

"Hello?' Mike answered.

She took a breath.

"Mike. Hi, it's Karen."   She hoped she wasn't bothering him.

"Oh, Hi Karen. I was just thinking about you."

She got a little excited at that thought.

"I was down at the Medical Examiner's office and Bill told me that there may be two different types of semen found on Sara. He's doing a match test and will know something in a day or two."

"Two huh? I wonder who the two are? You don't suppose it was Quinn and Stevens."

"Well, we'll know soon enough and if one isn't Josh, maybe that could be what we need to clear him."

"Maybe?" she asked.

"Well, there is still the murder. Just because she was raped doesn't mean the killer was the rapist, as far-fetched as it may seem, we have to look at it at all angles."

"But Stevens had the drug in his locker. So, he had access to it. So that may make him the main suspect."

"Well, until we get all the test results back, everyone at that party is a suspect."

She sighed. "Mike, are you....doing anything this evening?"

"I uh... don't really have any plans other than going over some paperwork and waiting on the results of the tests. Why? What do you have in mind?"

"How about a 7:30 movie? It will take our minds off work for a while."

"A movie sounds great! Just the distraction I need. I'll pick you up in 20 minutes."

He was going to pick her up? She was surprised. They always met at the places they went together. She threw on some makeup and did her hair in a flash. She picked out a casual but nice dress and although she had gotten ready at top speed, she looked very nice. Just as she was putting on her shoes, the doorbell rang. She opened the door and was expecting Mike but instead there was no one there. She looked around but there wasn't anyone in sight. Off in the distance, she heard tires screeching away. She thought that was odd but probably someone was trying to intimidate her.

After all, she was representing the main suspect in a murder case. She closed the door and went to Ann's room to tell her bye. Ann was on the phone with a friend.

"Ann, I'm going out to the movies with Mike. I'll be back later."

Ann smiled. "I won't wait up," she said with a grin. "Just in case you get lucky." Ann giggled and went back to talk on the phone.

Karen walked back to the living room and heard a car pull into the driveway. She looked out the window and saw Mike's car. She heard his car door shut and heard his footsteps coming towards the door. She waited for him to knock but he didn't. She was wondering what was keeping him from knocking and thought that maybe he was having second thoughts about them going out. Maybe he wants to keep everything at a professional level, she thought. She waited a moment longer and still no knock. She was getting impatient with him and wasn't going to wait any longer to find out why he wasn't knocking. She swung open the door yelling, "Mike, I got dressed and did my hair and makeup and if you think we're not going out now..........."

Mike was standing on her porch holding a knife in a handkerchief. She was shocked and gasped.

He didn't look up to her. He just stood there. He had a confused expression on his face. He finally looked up at her.

"You had a visitor."

She walked closer to him. "What?"

He held up the pocket knife. "This were stuck in your car tire."

She was frightened at the thought that someone would do such a thing.

"What is it?"

"It's a warning to keep your mouth shut."

Karen's eyes got wide. She looked at the knife in Mike's hand. She suddenly feared for her life.

"Does someone know about the tests we're having run? She asked

"I don't know. Who did you tell?" he asked her.

"I didn't tell anyone. Who did you tell?"

"Just Bill the medical examiner. He wouldn't say anything. He's an old friend of mine. As loyal as a dog. Plus, he knows everything is kept confidential until all the facts are in and then he tells the DA. Anyway, it's someone in the Marines."

"How do you know that?" she asked.

"This is a Marine tactical pocket knife."

Karen wasn't intimidated very easily. She was, however, worried about whether this person would do anything to Ann. She asked Ann if she wanted them to reschedule the movie and stay home, but Ann said she'd be okay. Karen made Ann promise she would call if anything unusual happened while they were gone. She made sure Ann turned the alarm on when she and Mike left.

The movie was a comedy. They both enjoyed it. She really needed a good laugh. After the movie, Karen gave Ann a quick call to check on things, then they went to get dessert at an ice cream shop. She was really enjoying herself with Mike. He didn't talk about business at all. He was casual. He even threw popcorn at her playfully at the movies. When she sat down at the table with her ice cream, she dropped her spoon on the floor. They both reached down to get it at the same time and his hand grabbed hers. For a moment, he held it. She was blushing. He smiled and let go of her hand. She sat up and he went to retrieve another spoon for her. She felt like a schoolgirl on her first date. She felt nervous and silly at the same time. She was a grown woman with an 18-year-old-daughter at home. She wasn't supposed to go ga-ga over guys anymore. That was for young inexperienced girls, not a 38-year-old attorney. But still, he sure made her feel nervous and excited at the same time. She watched him walk away and she caught a glimpse of his backside. She liked what she saw and blushed. He turned around and walked to her with a fresh clean spoon in his hand. She erased any inappropriate thoughts from her mind as he approached the table.

"Here you go, ma'am." He held the spoon out to her.

"Thanks!" she said with a smile.

He sat down and took a bite of his sundae. He thought for a moment.

"Karen, there's something I want to talk to you about." He looked around. "But not here, let's go for a walk."

Outside, the evening was warm and it felt good to Karen. In any other circumstance, her walking side by side with a handsome man at night would be romantic. But she knew Mike didn't think of her that way.

Mike remained quiet for a while. He seemed to be deep in thought as they walked. Karen was about to ask him what was on his mind when he spoke up.

"Karen, Jake has been gone for a long time."

"Yes. Over a year." She thought about the night she found out about Jake's car accident. It still made her shake. But she didn't want to talk about him at that moment. His memory was too painful.

"I know his death was hard on you. It was hard on me as well. He was my best friend, and a damn good detective." He grew silent in thought again.

"Mike, what's on your mind for you to bring up Jake?"

"This isn't easy for me to say. You know how I felt about Jake. It's just that.... It's been a year and a lot has happened between then and now and..... well, I was wondering, why do you still wear your wedding ring?"

Karen looked down at her left hand. It had been part of her for so long that the thought of not having it on seemed out of place.

She moved the ring around in her fingers.

"Oh, well, I thought about taking it off a lot. But I couldn't quite bring myself to do it just yet. I like having it close. I guess I really wasn't quite ready to let go of that piece of Jake yet."

"Karen, I know Jake would have wanted you to go on with your life, to find happiness again. That was the kind of guy we both know he was."

"I know."

"Karen, you do what feels right for you. Whenever you're ready, I can wait."

"What do you mean?"

They stopped walking. He gently grabbed her by the arm and held her close to him. He looked into her eyes. Her heart was beating wildly in her chest. He was so close. She almost lost her balance. His lips were just a few inches away from hers. She desperately wanted him to kiss her. He brushed her hair away from her face. His touch was so warm. It sent feelings of electricity throughout her body. He tilted her head back with his hand. He went to kiss her. She closed her eyes welcoming his kiss, but he stopped.

"I'm rushing, I'm sorry!" He said and took a step back.

She knew what he was talking about. She reached up and undid the gold chain she was wearing around her neck and slipped off her wedding ring. She placed it in the chain and Mike helped her put the necklace back on. She still was wearing it close, but she knew she had to move on. Mike held her chin in his hand and lifted her face to his. They kissed. The kiss was soft at first. His mouth was gentle. Then their passion inside was let out. She gave in to his embrace. He felt wonderful. She felt like she was floating towards heaven in his arms. She could have sworn that she was literally floating. She couldn't feel the ground. All she could feel was his lips on her and his hands on her back. After a moment of passion, he slowly pulled away from her lips. He looked into her eyes.

"I should get you home now."

She was a little let down. She didn't want to leave. She didn't want to stop kissing him. She wanted to go back to heaven in his arms.

"Home?"

"Yes. I want you to be safe. We still don't know who left you that message in your tire. Quinn and Stevens are in the brig so we know it wasn't them. It could be anyone. We need to be careful."

He was right. She still felt uneasy about the whole experience.

They drove to her home in silence. She wanted more of his kisses. She wanted to know who slashed her tire. She wanted to know who killed Sara Blake. Her head was spinning with questions and emotions. It was a big step for her to have removed her wedding ring.

She really needed to get some sleep. He walked her to the door.

"Do you want me to come in and check out the place?" he asked.

"No. The alarm is still active. I'll be fine." She did want him to come in. She wanted to spend the night with him more than she ever had before. But she knew it wasn't a good idea.

"I had a good time tonight." she said.

"Me too." He leaned down and kissed her. She put her arms around his waist as she kissed him back. Just then the porch light went on.

"We're being watched." Mike said.

Karen looked at the window by the front door and saw Ann duck back behind the curtain.

"She's just checking up on me, making sure I'm safe."

"You're very safe with me."

They kissed again and he pulled away slowly.

"Goodnight, Karen."

"Goodnight!"

She watched him walk back to his car and get in. She punched in her alarm code and went inside and locked the door behind her. Ann was standing there waiting for her mother to speak.

"Well, how did it go?"

"Oh, you know. You were watching from that window."
Ann smiled.

"I was just seeing if you were being treated well."

"Yes, I was." Karen said. "Mike was a perfect gentleman."

"Well, were you a perfect lady?"

Karen rolled her eyes. "Go to bed young lady!"

Ann smiled. "Goodnight, Mom." She headed up to her room.

Karen reset the alarm and went up to bed. She couldn't sleep. Her thoughts were on Mike and their kiss. She had wanted him to stay the night.

She was drifting off to sleep when the phone rang. She sleepily reached for it.

"Mike?"

She heard no one.

"Hello?"

No noise except for someone's breathing.

"Who is this?"

"Keep your mouth shut!" someone whispered. Then they hung up.

Chapter Ten

S tevens was led to the room where Karen waited to interview him. He didn't smile like Quinn had. He looked like someone who didn't quite know what was going on. He sat down across from her. She held out her hand to shake. "Tim, I'm JAG Officer Karen Stuart. I'm representing Second Lieutenant Josh O'Riley. I need to ask you a few questions."

He looked at her as if he was looking right through her. It chilled her.

"I told the police everything. I didn't do it." he said.

She looked at him. She couldn't tell whether he was lying or telling the truth.

"I want you to tell me what you know. If you tell me what you know, it could get you free. But you have to be honest with me here."

He looked down and nodded his head.

She pushed record on her micro-recorder.

"Now, please tell me about the party."

Stevens leaned forward in his seat. He was silent for a moment then began.

"Me and Quinn rode together to the party. I think it was about 6:30 or so when we got there. Josh decided to go to the commissary and said he would meet us at the party soon after. When me and Quinn got to Amanda's, we immediately hit the beer and just goofed off with the guys."

"Tell me about when you and Quinn went into the house."

"Well, I guess Sara was feeling pretty sick or something. So, Josh helped her into the house. I guess just to help her lay down. Anyway, we figured we would wait for Josh to come out to ask him if she was okay. But a couple of minutes later he hadn't come out and we were worried about Sara, so we went in. He was in the bathroom. We decided to head upstairs to see if Sara was okay. We could tell by the way she had been acting before that she may have drunk too much. She seemed okay, just resting. Well, I know Quinn told you it was my idea to take the picture of Sara passed out, but it wasn't me. He was the one who wanted to get back at Arthur because of the picture he had shown his girlfriend."

Stevens giggled. "Yeah, that was pretty funny. Quinn's girlfriend was so mad at him, but she thought it was funny too. Anyway, when we got to the bedroom, Sara was out cold. He pulled out his cell phone and took a picture. Then we heard someone come into the house so we left and went back to the party. Quinn doesn't know, but later, after we came back to the barracks, I grabbed his phone while he was in the bathroom and I deleted the photo we took. I felt bad about it right after we did it, but I knew Quinn wasn't going to delete it himself. Well, we left the party a little later and that is all I knew until we were arrested the next day. I tell you; we didn't have anything to do with that. All we did was take a stupid picture of Sara. I swear! Someone else did it and is letting me, Quinn and O'Riley take the blame."

Karen leaned in. "You don't believe that O'Riley did it?"

"Him and Quinn had some arguments as some roommates do but O'Riley is a good guy. He's like a big teddy bear. He wouldn't have hurt Sara. Not as much as he cared for her."

"What do you mean?"

Stevens hesitated for a moment, then began to explain.

"O'Riley had feelings for Sara, I think. I could tell by the way that he acted when she talked to him. I think she may have had some feelings for him as well but I couldn't tell for sure. I just had the feeling that they secretly felt a little something for each other."

"Do you think that anything had ever happened between them?"

"No, other than maybe some discreet flirting. I know that she loved Blake very much and she was very loyal to him. I would bet my life on that."

Karen didn't know why, but she was getting the feeling that Stevens was telling the truth. He seemed honest. She didn't know whether to trust those feelings or not.

"Stevens, tell me about the drugs found in your locker at work."

He looked up at her in surprise. He didn't know how she knew about that.

"How did you...?"

"I'm an attorney. I make it my business to get all the facts. Now, please tell me about that. Why did you have them in your locker and what happened to them after Major Murphy took them away?"

He sank into his seat with a look of shame. He paused before he answered her.

"I wanted to try them because someone I had met on a deployment told me they helped you when you are having trouble sleeping. I was having insomnia.

Maybe too much caffeine before bed. I don't want to fly feeling so tired during the day. So, I got a hold of some from a guy. Someone who isn't in the Marines. That's all I'm going to tell you about that! Anyway, I was nervous about taking them because I didn't want to have a drug test after I took one. I was going to throw them away but Blake had found them before I got the chance. He went to Major Murphy. Major Murphy said that he wouldn't report me to the authorities if I just turned over the pills and never spoke about them again. So I did. I was restricted for a week from flying until I took a urine test. I passed so he let me fly again. Then one day Major Murphy storms in the chow hall and demands someone tell him who broke into his desk. No one knew what he was talking about. I didn't know anything about anyone doing that. I only know that's where he had put the pills. I didn't want them so why would I steal them back? I hated being grounded. I love to fly. It's all I've always loved to do."

"So, they never showed up?"

"Nope!"

"Do you know who may have stolen them?"

"I have no idea. As far as I had known, he was the only one that knew about them, well besides me and Blake."

"One more question. Did you see anyone go back in the house after you and Quinn came out at the party?"

He thought for a moment. "No. Amanda locked the house back up. I don't think anyone else knows the combination."

"I think I have all I need. But if not, I may be back."

They shook hands and she left. She was glad that that interview wasn't like she thought it was going to be. She wondered how someone like Stevens would be hanging out with someone like Quinn. She thought that maybe Stevens wasn't as bright as he seemed.

The court-martial was slowly approaching. Mike and Karen were sitting in his office discussing how time until the trial was getting closer when the phone rang.

"Mike speaking."

"Mike, it's Bill. I don't know how you knew, but you were right. Her body had traces of the drug GHB, also known as the date rape drug. You might want to come down and we could talk more about it. I'm glad you thought of it or I would have never thought to look for it. It's so hard to trace. I also have the results of the semen tests. We need to discuss that."

Mike cut him off. "I'm on my way now." and he put down the phone.

Karen had seen the look on Mike's face and was confused, until he told her what Bill had said.

They both high-tailed it to the coroner's office in ten minutes.

Bill was sitting at his desk when the two of them charged in.

"Well, was it the GHB that killed her?" Mike asked.

Bill looked up at them in surprise that they had gotten there so fast.

"She had enough in her system to cause respiratory distress, although she had some alcohol in her system as well, it was very little. The amount of GHB in her system is what caused her to stop breathing.

Mike and Karen looked at each other. Arthur's help was more than he could have known. Cause of death, GHB. Now they just had to find out who gave it to Sara. But first, Mike and Karen needed to know the semen test results.

"Bill, the semen test results. Tell me how it turned out."
Bill reached on his desk and picked up a file.

"I was shocked at the results. I thought that there was an error somewhere so I ran it twice. That's what took so long." He handed the file to Mike who looked through the results with a shocked expression. He looked up at Bill.

"This can't be right!" he said.

"It's right. None of the three young men's semen tests matched those found on Sara Blake."

"What?" Karen said in shock. "That can't be right! That means that..."

"That means," Bill interrupted, "That as far as the rape goes, Quinn, Stevens and O'Riley are innocent. You just find out who gave Sara the GHB and you'll find the rapist and murderer."

Mike and Karen looked at each other. Karen was looking through the test results for any mistake, then put down the file onto Bill's desk.

"This clears O'Riley, Quinn and Stevens of the rape, but there's still the murder. Somehow, I don't know how, we have to find out where that missing bottle of pills went."

They both headed out the door as Bill said goodbye.

Mike turned around. "Thanks Bill. You've helped more than you know."

"I can't believe it! Karen said as they were walking back to the car. "I can't believe we would've missed it if we hadn't talked to Arthur."

"It just goes to show you that you never know what will pop up in a case like this. Thankfully Arthur remembered the pills. If he hadn't, we would be looking at this all wrong."

Arthur woke up quickly. He thought he heard a noise in his room. He looked around but it was too dark. He saw a shadow. It didn't move at first. But then it slowly came closer to him. It was hard to make out at first, but it was a figure of a man. Arthur thought it was one of the nurses coming to give him his sleeping pill. But they always woke him up. This person was being quiet so as to not be seen or heard. Arthur was about to speak, but he thought that maybe he should let the man think that he was asleep. He wanted to watch and see what the man was up to.

The figure came closer. The man wore dark clothing and it was much too dark to see his face. Arthur watched him carefully, not moving.

The man came even closer. Arthur could see something in the man's hand. The dim light from the street caused a flicker of light to reflect on the metal object in the man's hand. When the man came even closer and was standing over Arthur's bed, he saw that it was a syringe that the man was holding. Arthur ever so slowly reached for the call button by his bed. The man moved over to Arthur's IV bag and Arthur watched as the man emptied the contents of the syringe in his IV just as Arthur hit the call button. The man, realizing that Arthur was awake, dropped the needle, ran to the opened window and quickly jumped out. The drug started to move quickly into Arthur's bloodstream and he started to lose consciousness just as a nurse rushed into the room. She turned on the lights and looked at Arthur, who could only point towards the open window, and then she noticed the syringe on the floor. She quickly pulled out the IV needle from his arm, hoping to stop any more of the syringe's contents from entering his bloodstream. She made sure his vitals were normal, then she went to call the police.

Major Murphy came out of the elevator on the second floor of the hospital. He walked towards Arthur Blake's room that was buzzing with police. He saw Mike talking with a nurse. Major Murphy approached them.

"Agent Mike Walker! Here again huh? What's the special occasion?"

Mike stopped his interview with the nurse who saved Blake and turned to Major Murphy.

"Officer, someone came to visit Mr. Blake around midnight last night. He left him a present in his IV. Morphine. A pretty deadly dose. Thankfully Mr. Blake was able to hit the call button and the nurse came in and took out the IV just in time. The visitor took off out the window just before the nurse came in. He left the syringe, but no fingerprints. He had to be wearing gloves."

Major Murphy looked shocked and angered. "Is Captain Blake ok?"

"Yes, luckily. He's just been a little out of it. He'll be fine in a while. I'm surprised to see you didn't know about this."

"What do you mean?" Major Murphy asked.

"Well, you've been here so often, watching out like a hawk, making sure no one gets too close to him. Guess you can't be everywhere at once, right?"

"I check up on him from time to time but I would hardly say I watch over him like a hawk, Mr. Walker. Isn't it your responsibility to find out who did it? Isn't that your job? Well, right now my responsibility is to make sure my guy is taken well care of so he can get back in the air where he wants to be. What about you? Have you done your job and found out who raped and killed Sara?"

Mike paused for a moment. Major Murphy was getting under his skin.

"Well, actually Officer, the semen tests came back negative on all three of them. So, someone else is responsible for the rape at least."

The Officer's expression hardened. "That must be a mistake. No one else was in the house except those three Marines. It had to be O'Riley. His dog tags were in her hand. He murdered that dear girl. You just missed something. You need to go back over your evidence, Agent Walker!"

"And you, Major Murphy, need to keep your nose out of my work and let us professionals do our job." Mike was irate. "Where were you last night Major?" Mike asked sharply.

Before Major Murphy could respond, they were interrupted.

"Major Murphy! I was wondering when you would show up again." The doctor said as he walked up behind Major Murphy. "I guess you heard the awful news about last night's visitor."

"Yes I did Dr. White. CID Agent Walker and I were just discussing it. He's going to be a hero and crack the case, aren't you Agent Walker?"

Mike wanted to slug Major Murphy.

"I'm here to do my job!"

"Well, no more questioning my patient." Dr White said. "He's very distraught about what happened last night. Asking him more questions is only going to make it worse for him."

"Don't worry Doctor, I won't be bothering him anymore. I got exactly all I needed here."

Chapter Eleven

"I can't believe someone tried to kill Arthur." Karen was saying to Mike as they were going through some paperwork. His living room was covered with papers of statements from witnesses.

"Well, someone doesn't want him to talk. The same someone who doesn't want you to talk. Are you still getting those phone calls?"

Karen sighed. "Yes! I thought I might have recognized the voice. Definitely an older male. What does this person think I know?"

Mike scratched his head as he paced back and forth.

"Well, whatever they think you know, they think I must know as well because I've been getting the calls too."

Karen looked up at him. "You too?"

"Yep!"

"Well, at least I'm not the only one being woken up at night by some wacko."

Mike smiled.

Karen looked through the papers in front of her and in her hand.

"There's got to be more here. Something that will tell us who raped and killed Sara. Or at least point us in the right direction."

Just then Karen's cell phone rang.

"Hello!"

"Hi, Ms. Stewart? Sorry to bother you." Karen recognized the voice. It was Amanda.

"It's me, Amanda. You asked me to call you if I remembered anything. Well, there may be something that I forgot to mention to you. I just remembered it. Can we meet somewhere?"

"Yes! Of course. I'm at Agent Mike Walker's house right now. Here's the address."

Amanda sat on the chair opposite of Mike and Karen. She looked a little nervous.

"Would you like something to drink?" Mike asked her.

"No thanks." She said with a half-smile.

Karen leaned in closer to her.

"Amanda. O'Riley, Quinn and Stevens are cleared of the rape, but they are still under suspicion of the murder. There's a court-martial we need to stop from happening. If there is anything you know that can help us find out who killed Sara, anything at all, please tell us."

Amanda nodded her head. After a moment, she spoke up.

"When you questioned me before about what I saw when I was in the house that night, I forgot to mention something. I don't like texting so I decided I'd just call you. I remember that I saw there was a tissue with dark pink lipstick on it in the bathroom trash can. It was the shade Sara was wearing that evening. I don't wear lipstick so I know it wasn't mine. I wear lip gloss from time to time but never lip stick. I found it strange since O'Riley was the only one who went into that bathroom that night, other than me. He said he went into the bathroom after taking her to the guest room."

Karen looked at Mike. "He didn't mention anything about seeing something like that when he was in there."

"I know it's probably nothing, but it makes no sense to me why Sara would bother with wiping off her lipstick when she wasn't feeling well. She just wanted to lay down. The rest of her makeup was on her face the next morning. So why the lipstick? I'm sorry! It's probably nothing. I'm sorry if I'm wasting your time."

"It's not nothing Amanda." Mike interrupted. "Anything, even a small detail may help solve this case."

"Right! time is slowly running out and even tiny details we missed before could be what we need to get these boys off the hook."

Amanda smiled. "I don't think these three pilots hurt her. I'd almost bet my own life on it. I hope you can prove he is innocent."

Karen looked at Mike and back at Amanda.

"We do too!"

The next day, Amanda went to go visit Arthur at the hospital. She hadn't seen him since the night before he left for Japan. She knew he must have questions for her since the incident happened at her house. He was sitting up in bed trying to listen in on a news broadcast on the television in the next room. He was trying to find out anything about his wife's murder. He was surprised when he saw Amanda walk in.

"Amanda?"

"Hey Blake!" She came in and sat down in the chair by his bed.

"How did you get past the nurses? They've been watching me like a hawk." Amanda and Arthur both looked over at the nurse station. They seemed to be busy, not paying them any attention.

"You look like hell!" She said, teasing him. She was trying to act normal to cheer him up. She didn't want to seem so serious. She knew he didn't want to be coddled.

"Well considering I'm in it, it's an appropriate look for me I guess."

"The guys at work are asking about you, ya know. They want to come visit you but they aren't sure you'd be up for it." He sighed.

"I'm not ready to see anyone yet. Everyone who was at the party, I work with. So, when I go back to work and I see all their faces, I'm going to feel so much rage. Why didn't someone watch out for Sara?"

"You mean me?" She asked. He thought for a moment.

"You were the first person I was angry with. It was your party. It happened in your house. I couldn't understand how this all happened. But I also know you had no way of knowing that anything like that was going to happen. So, no. I'm not blaming you. Not anymore." She smiled.

"Do you know anything about what happened? Have they told you anything?" she asked him.

"No. just basic stuff, but no details. They don't want to upset me. As if anything else could top what I'm going through already." He looked up at her. "What about you? Do you know much about what they've found out?"

"No. I really don't want to see these guys get convicted. I don't think our friends would have done any of this. It doesn't make sense to me."

"Yeah. I don't think they did anything that would hurt Sara. It's got to be someone else! But who? Who would want to hurt Sara? I just wish I knew if she had been drugged. I'd like to think she wasn't conscious through her attack."

"Drugged? Why do you think that?" Amanda was caught off guard with that statement.

"Well, I know I'm not supposed to talk about any of the details with anyone, but I know I can trust you!"

Arthur explained to her about the GHB he found on Stevens, and how they were in an old film container. He also told her about how they turned up missing from Major Murphy's locker. "If we could find out where the pills are, and she was in fact drugged, we'd probably know the son of a bitch who did this to Sara." Amanda looked concerned. She looked like she was about to cry. She leaned in and softly spoke. "Blake, I think I know who has the pills."

Amanda stood on the porch. She hesitated before ringing the doorbell. She was wearing a dress. Something she never liked to do. She had her hair done and makeup on, which made her look very feminine and attractive. Dresses were definitely not her thing, but she had to do this. She took a deep breath before she knocked on the door.

She waited a moment and when he didn't answer the door, she said to herself in a whisper, "This is crazy."

Just then the door opened. She smiled.

"Amanda! You look fantastic!" The man said as he eyed her up and down.

"Thanks! I just thought we could have that night cap you've been asking me for."

His eyes lit up. A devilish grin appeared on his mouth.

"Sure, come in!"

She forced herself to smile as she walked past him into the room. He looked around outside the hall to see if anyone was watching and then he closed the door.

"Hey Bill! I've got something for you." Mike said as he came into the Medical Examiner's office. Bill looked up at his friend and smiled.

"Mike, how have you been? Did you find out who the killer was yet?"

"No, but that's why I'm here. Match this up with the sample found on Sara." Mike handed him a vile with a liquid in it. "Can you do it ASAP?"

Bill took the vial from Mike's hand. "Just watch the pro do his magic."

"Bill, I need another favor from you."

Bill smiled. "Whatever it is, I'll do it. As long as it's legal."

"Great!" Mike said. "Come with me! There's someone at the hospital on base I would like you to meet."

Karen went to see Josh again. She needed to know what really happened in the five minutes he was in the house with Sara. She needed an explanation of the lipstick on the tissue. She sat down at the table across from him and without saying a word, she took out her micro-recorder, pushed record and sat back and looked at him.

"Josh. If you want to get out of here, you have to tell me everything. I will do my best to get you out, but you have to help me. What happened in those five minutes? And why were your dog tags in Sara's room? Don't give me any bullshit this time. Be straight with me!"

He sighed and sank in his chair. For a moment, he was silent, debating whether or not to tell her the truth. He was afraid of the consequences.

"Josh? How about you tell me about the lipstick on the tissue in the bathroom trash." He looked up at her, shocked. He had no idea she knew about that.

"Josh, either you tell me now or the judge is going to drag it out of you at your court-martial in front of everyone present!"

"Okay!" he finally said. "I'll tell you. But I don't want Blake to know."

"Know what?" He hesitated.

"Josh!" Know what? Talk to me!"

He kept his gaze down on the table at the micro-recorder. "Does that have to be on? He asked her.

She ignored the question.

"What happened in that room, Josh?" she persisted, even more sternly. "Amanda said she found a tissue with lipstick in her bathroom trash. She doesn't wear lipstick so she knew you had something you weren't saying about when you were alone with Sara. You were the only one, besides Amanda who was in that bathroom that evening. So, tell me the truth! What happened in the bedroom?"

"I didn't mean for it to happen," he pleaded with her. "I helped her into the house, up the stairs and into the guest room"

"Then what happened?"

"She began to cry. I felt really bad. I knew it was because Blake had just left for six months and she was sad about it. She didn't have any family around and I think she was feeling scared about being alone. So I let her cry on my shoulder. I reached into my pocket to see if I had a tissue to wipe her tears. The dog tags must have fallen out then."

He stopped and took a deep breath and looked down again at the micro-recorder.

"What happened then?"

"We didn't mean for it to happen, it just did."

"What happened Josh?" He looked up at her. "She pulled me in and kissed me. It just happened so fast. She seemed not like herself at all. Like she was totally drunk, not realizing what she was doing. As soon as I realized what was going on, I pulled away. I helped her lay down, covered her up and told her to get some sleep. She was laughing and she called me Arthur. I realized she probably didn't even know who I was at that moment and wasn't going to remember what had just happened, so I just walked out of the room, closed the door behind me and let her rest." He started to tear up.

"What's Blake gonna think?"

"Josh, I don't think you comforting his upset wife would make him mad, considering what someone else had done to her."

"I know, but I'm supposed to be his best friend. Some friend I am. And Ann. What's she gonna think about me now?"

So that's why you weren't up front with me before? Because you thought Arthur or Ann would be mad about Sara kissing you?"

"Yes."

She sighed.

After a moment, Karen said, "Well that explains what happened in the five minutes you were in the house, and the dog tags. But how did they end up in her hand?"

"I have no idea! I'm not even sure where I had dropped them. Someone must have placed them in her hand as some sick joke, or to frame me." Karen could tell he was very upset. It didn't seem like he was acting.

"Josh, tell me what happened then, after you left her in the room?"

"I headed to the bathroom to think for a moment. I couldn't believe what had just happened. I needed to process it. I noticed in the mirror that I had lipstick on my face from Sara's kiss. So, I grabbed a tissue, wiped off all I could and threw it in the trash. That's what I was doing in the bathroom. I know I told you before I was just rehearsing my proposal to Ann, which isn't completely untrue. I've been rehearsing for weeks, but not at that moment. I needed to clear my head. I was so afraid that somehow Blake would find out so I took a few minutes to calm down, wipe off the lipstick and compose myself. That's what I was doing when I ran into Amanda outside of the bathroom. I tried so hard to play it cool. Then I headed out to the party."

Karen looked at him curiously. "Just how long did this kiss last?"

He looked ashamed. "It was longer than I care to admit to. But I put a stop to it! Please don't tell Ann. It didn't mean anything. Neither one of us meant it to happen and I ended it right away. Nothing more happened. I swear! I would never cheat on Ann. I love her. And I know that Sara loved Blake more than life itself. It was just a terrible mistake. I didn't want to say anything about it before because I was ashamed."

He was upset. She could tell by the way he was acting that his words were sincere.

She placed her hand on his. "Josh, I know you didn't mean for that to happen. I know you wouldn't purposely hurt Ann."

"She'll know about this won't she? Blake will know too huh? I might as well stay locked up. The two people who mean the world to me, I betrayed."

"Josh, Sara wasn't herself at that moment. It sounds like you handled it like any honest guy would. You didn't force her to kiss you. Don't be so hard on yourself. I will explain it to Ann. She will understand, so will Captain Blake."

He looked up at her, wanting to believe her words.

"Do you really think that is how it will be?" "Absolutely. Honesty is always the best way. Be honest! It will be the best thing to do, you'll see."

He let out a small smile and wiped the tears away that had run down his face.

He nodded.

Major Murphy was talking to Gunny Brown in the hallway of the hanger when an MP walked up to him.

"Sir, are you Major Tom Murphy?" the officer asked him.

Without answering the man, Major Murphy said, "What's this all about?"

The MP saw Major Murphy's name on his uniform and handed him the envelope in his hand.

"Sir, this is for you." and the MP walked off.

Major Murphy eyed the envelope for a moment. He didn't know what it could be. He opened it up and read the letter inside. It was a subpoena to testify at O'Riley's court-martial. They're going to question him on the witness stand. "Damn it!" he said out loud. Gunny Brown looked at him strangely.

"Major, is everything alright?" he asked.

Major Murphy sighed and looked at him.

"Well, it's a subpoena to testify at O'Riley's court-martial!"

"Well, that shouldn't be a problem, right? You have nothing to hide!"

Major Murphy looked at him and then down at the letter.

"Sir, I need to go somewhere. I'll be back in an hour." Officer Murphy quickly walked away.

"Where are you going?" Gunny Brown asked him. He didn't answer.

Karen told Ann bye and got in her car. She was on her way to Mike's. She turned on the radio and was singing to it. It was one of her favorite songs. She was in a good mood. She and Mike had dinner reservations at Mario's restaurant. It was quite an expensive restaurant, but it was a special occasion. They were so close to solving the case that Mike wanted to do something fun.

He had actually even called it a date. She was thrilled. Where is this relationship going? she thought to herself. He had kissed her and that was wonderful, but he hadn't since that night. Was he having second thoughts about taking their relationship further? She hoped this date would answer that question. She was too busy thinking about her and Mike that she didn't notice the car behind her was following her the whole way. She finally glanced in her rearview mirror and noticed the car just as she was pulling into Mike's driveway. The car went on by and she couldn't see who was driving. She thought that she was just being paranoid and went to the door and knocked. Mike opened the door. He was in a casual dress shirt and black jeans.

"Wow! You look terrific!" he said when he saw her. She had her hair and makeup done and she was wearing a red sundress that accentuated her figure. She smiled at him.

"Thanks, you look nice yourself. I can't remember seeing you in jeans for a long time. They look nice on you." He grinned.

"Are you ready?"

"Yep."

"Okay, let's take my car."

As they drove to the restaurant, Mike noticed Karen kept looking behind them.

"Karen, what are you looking at?"

She turned back around and faced the front.

"Well, on my way to your house, I could have sworn I was being followed. And just a minute ago, the same car was behind us. Now it's hard to see if he's still there."

It had gotten dark out and she only saw the headlights from the car behind them.

"It's probably just your nerves. This whole case has had that effect on me too."

"Well, the phone calls have stopped. I guess it's alright   now."
"Yeah, whoever it was probably found something better to do than bother us. Now here we are. No more talking about the case."

They pulled into a parking space at the restaurant and got out. She looked back to see if any cars were following them. She saw none so they went in.

The dinner was great. Even though it was a bit pricey, Mike told her to order whatever she wanted, so she ordered the lobster. He had the same.

During dinner, he talked about how he felt he had jumped the gun and kissed her too early.

"I shouldn't have kissed you like that. I was Jake's best friend. I shouldn't try to make a move on his wife."

"Mike, I'm no longer his wife. It's been long enough for me to get my life back together and start living. I have put that off for too long and if he could communicate with us, I'm sure he would approve of me dating you. In fact, there's no one else I could possibly think of that he would approve of more."

Mike smiled. "If it's alright, I would like to take you out more often."

She smiled and put her hand on his. "I would love that, Mike. Just as long as we take things slow, and see what happens."

After dinner they got back in the car and started for his place. Karen was calmer and had forgotten all about the car she had seen following her earlier until the car behind them bumped them. Mike almost lost control of the car. The car behind them bumped them again.

"Hold on!" Mike yelled at her.

He tried to get a look at who was behind them. It looked like a man, but they couldn't see who. It was too dark to tell. Mike grabbed the wheel and gained control of the car. Then the car behind them moved up beside them. It was an expensive looking black luxury car. They couldn't see the make. They could see that the culprit wore a mask. It was a black ski mask. The man in the mask pushed into Mike's car from the side. They were knocked out of the road and into a ditch. They came to a stop. They tried to get the license plate of the man as he sped away. Mike only got the first five numbers. LAN-47.

"Are you alright?" he asked Karen.

She nodded, still in shock. It had all happened so fast. Too fast for either of them to really know what was going on until it was over. Someone was trying very hard to scare them. Probably the same one who left the knife in Karen's tire and the same one who had been calling them both with threats.

Mike got out of the car and looked at it. They had a flat tire. As he went to the trunk and grabbed the tire wrench and jack, he noticed Karen on her cell phone.

"Who are you calling?"

"A friend of mine at the DMV. I'm going to have her run a list of people who have license plates on vehicles that might match the one that just ran us off the road. I'll give her the numbers we got off the license plate. It's a long shot I know, but it's a place to start."

Mike sighed. "As soon as I hear back from Bill and it turns out the way I think it will, I'll have all I need for an arrest." He sighed. "I sure hope I can do that before one of us gets hurt by this madman."

Mike had just got home from work. He had been sweating bullets waiting for that DNA test to come back. Karen was on edge wanting to get Josh free and he had almost all he needed to make an arrest. He was so close yet so far away. He hit the play button on his answering machine. Three were hang-ups, and the fourth was Bill.

"Hey Mike, I have something that might interest you. Call me as soon as you can."

The message ended.

"The DNA results!" Mike whispered to himself.

He picked up his phone and called Bill.

Bill answered on the second ring.

"This is Bill, talk to me!"

"Bill, it's Mike."

"Mike! I was expecting you to call me fast and you sure did. I left that message for you only five minutes ago. I have the results of the test you wanted me to run."

Mike was aware that his messages were still playing. He could hear them in the background as Bill was about to tell him the results, he told him to hold on a second. He listened as he heard Karen's voice on the answering machine.

"Mike! My friend from the DMV got back to me. She has that list of cars with those matching numbers on the tags and she faxed it to you earlier." Mike walked over to his fax machine and picked up the fax. He was shocked at what he saw.

"I'm driving. I got a text message from Amanda that she needed to see me about something important and to meet her at her house. It's funny because she said she hated texting. Oh well, I'm on my way there now. Give me a call when you get this message. Bye."

Mike came back to the phone with Bill, He heard Bill say "We have a positive." He couldn't believe it.

"Mike! Did you hear me?" Bill was saying as Mike was trying to process the results. "It was a positive on him."

Mike had heard him. "Bill, did you tell anyone about the test results yet?" There was a pause.

"No. I haven't. Why?"

"Oh no!" he said.

"Mike! Are you there?" Bill was yelling on the other end of the phone.

Mike ran to the phone and picked it up.

"Bill, I'm on my way over to Amanda's now. She and Karen might be in danger! I'll explain later!"

Mike picked up his cell phone as he drove. He dialed Karen's number, but no answer.

"Come on Karen, pick up!" he said angrily above a whisper.

After seven rings and no answer, Mike stepped on the gas even harder.

Ten minutes later, he was at Amanda's house. He quickly parked and ran to the door. It was unlocked. He reached for his gun under his jacket and slowly stepped inside. He heard voices down a hallway. He made his way down the hall towards the voices. As he got closer, it sounded more like muffled voices rather than a conversation. Before he reached the closed door, he saw a movement out of the corner of his eye. He turned and saw Karen walking up to him.

"Mike, what's going on?" she asked as she saw he was standing with his gun drawn.

"Mike! What are you doing here?" He turned to see Karen standing behind him with a confused expression on her face.

"Karen, I thought you were in trouble. I thought I heard a muffled scream."

"I didn't scream. I don't know what you heard. Anyway, what are you doing here?"

"Well," he said as he put his gun back in his jacket. "Bill called me and while we were on the phone, I heard your message being played. I saw the fax from your friend and that's when I knew you were in danger."

"In danger? Of what?"

"It wasn't Josh, it wasn't Quinn or Stevens." He spoke.

"What do you mean?" she asked.

Just then they both heard a noise coming from the closed door. It was a muffled scream.

"Amanda?" Karen yelled.

Mike opened the door and he and Karen ran in to see a man holding a gun to Amanda's head. The man had one hand over her mouth so she couldn't scream. The man with the gun wore a mask. Mike and Karen, both recognized it. It was that same black ski mask the man was wearing that ran them off the road. Karen gasped.

"Come any closer and she dies." the voice under the mask said.

Karen was terrified. She was too scared to move.

Mike put his hands up. "Major Murphy, let her go!"

"Major Murphy?" Karen asked.

The man pulled off his mask and threw it on the floor. "So Detective, I guess you do know your job!"

Major Murphy made a boyish face as if he were caught with his hand in the cookie jar.

Karen stood in shock at the sight of Major Murphy standing with a gun to Amanda's head.

"Please don't hurt her." Karen pleaded with him.

Mike took a step forward. Major Murphy saw him and pushed the gun even closer to her head.

"Now Agent Walker, don't be stupid." he said.

"Mike, how did you know it was Major Murphy?" Karen asked, confused.

"Well, I'll explain it to you and to the Major." Mike looked right at Major Murphy. "You see, I first had my suspicion of you at the hospital when you mentioned O'Riley's dog tags being found in Sara's hand. No one other than those involved with the crime scene and the investigation knew about the dog tags, but you not only mentioned them, you knew they were O'Riley's and that they were in her hand. That was not released to the public. Yet you knew. You couldn't have known that information unless you were at the crime scene." Major Murphy didn't speak.

Karen was in tears. She was confused at what was going on.

"You raped and killed Sara? It was you?" Karen asked, still in shock.

"I didn't rape her. She wanted it! She was always acting like she wasn't interested in me, but I could tell. I just wanted her to loosen up a bit. Then she wouldn't be so uptight and she'd finally give in to her longing."

"What? She didn't want that! You're sick!" Karen asked.

"No. You don't understand at all. I never meant for her to get hurt. I was just getting her in a state of relaxation. I loved her!"

"You're not well, Major. Please put the gun down. We can get you some help!"

"Oh, Agent Walker, I'm perfectly sane. I'm the top dog around base. That's right! I have the authority to pull some strings, to get things cleared up. So go ahead, tell her what you found out, Mr. Detective. It doesn't matter because no one will believe I did anything to that girl!" Major Murphy gave Mike a glare.

Mike looked at Major Murphy and without ever taking his eyes off him, he began to speak.

"Well, Major, the way I imagine that it happened was this. You had a thing for Sara. Made advances to her every now and then when Captain Blake wasn't around. But she loved her husband and she wouldn't ever do anything to betray him like that. So, she turned you down. But that made you angry. You were desperate to have your way. You knew that Amanda would have her shop party before the squadron's deployment to Japan, so you purposely sent Captain Blake out as advance party so he would be out of the way. Then you talked Amanda into inviting Sara, to cheer her up as you put it. So, when she showed up and asked for a drink, you offered to bring her one. Only it wasn't just a drink you were bringing her, was it? You had slipped GHB into her drink. Too much actually. You waited for the drug to take effect and for her to say she was tired. I believe your plan was to offer to take Sara inside to the spare bedroom upstairs to take advantage of her being out of it. But when you saw O'Riley take her inside to lie down, you knew you had to think up another plan. You would have to wait til the coast was clear and go upstairs to find her sleeping and unable to fight you off. Only you didn't know that GHB mixed with alcohol could be dangerous, did you Major?" The Major's expression changed to confusion.

When Major Murphy didn't say anything, Mike continued.

"You waited for your chance to go upstairs to Sara, but Josh had been a gentleman and took her to the room first to lay down for a while. You waited for him to come out to make your way up to her but he didn't come right out. Then you saw Quinn and Stevens go in. They knew something wasn't right with her but they had no idea she was drugged so they went back to the party. Then Amanda went in and checked on her and found her asleep, but she wasn't really just taking a nap at that time, she had slipped into unconsciousness by then due to the drugs. A few hours later, the party had died down a little. Somewhere around 9:30 you decided now was your chance. So, you made up this lie about how you were going for beer, only no one I interviewed saw or heard you drive away. That's because you didn't go to the store, you went in through the side of the house.

The padlock was on the door, but you knew the combination, didn't you? I mean after all; you and Amanda had been having a secret affair. You put on gloves so there were no fingerprints left on the lock. So, you went into the house and quickly went upstairs to where Sara lay alone and unconscious and you raped her. She was out cold. You knew that was the only way she couldn't turn you down. When you were done, you must have thought that she would notice what had happened to her when she would wake up the next morning, so trying to think quickly, you found O'Riley's dog tags on the floor and placed them in her hand. You probably thought she would assume she had been attacked by O'Riley. So, then you quickly went back outside, put the pad lock back on the door, reset the lock, went out front to your car where you had an ice cooler full of beer cans and half-melted ice by that time. You didn't want to come back to the party without the beer you supposedly left to go get."

Major Murphy began to laugh. "Well Agent Walker. You're not as smart as you think you are. I didn't kill Sara. She was alive when I saw her. I only used a small amount of GHB to relax her. So, I'm not a murderer."

"I'm guessing you didn't know that GHB mixed with alcohol can be deadly to someone Sara's size. She was dead Major. The Medical examiner put her time of death right around 8:15 pm that night. You came to Sara around 9:30!" Major Murphy's expression grew cold. His eyes widened. "No. That can't be. She was sleeping!"

"It only appeared that way because she was in bed and it was dark."

"No, that's not possible! She wasn't…..I didn't…" Major Murphy looked sick. His face went white.

"Was she warm? Did she speak, moan, move? Think about it!"

Major Murphy was speechless. He just stared at Mike.

"The only thing positive about the situation is the fact that she wasn't alive to suffer through what you did to her!"

Karen, who was shocked at the whole account, looked back at Mike.

"How did you get a semen sample of him to run?" Karen asked

"Well, After Amanda came to us a few days ago and confessed she had been seeing him secretly, she took it upon herself to find out the truth about her suspicions that maybe he was involved with the crime." He looked back at Major Murphy. "Amanda, went to your house and slept with you. While you were asleep, she took the condom you had used, put it in a plastic bag and snuck out. Then she took the semen sample right over to me. I then took it to the Medical Examiner to run a comparison to that sample found on Sara."

"Oh, you sneaky back-stabbing bitch!" Major Murphy said to Amanda. She didn't move, but gave him a hateful look. He turned back to Mike."

Mike kept his eyes on Major Murphy. But spoke to Karen. "I was on the phone with Bill getting the results when I heard your message about the DMV list. Guess what I found, Major?" Major Murphy, no longer smiling, answered.

"You tell me detective!" He was looking concerned.

"It was an exact match. But I didn't know for a fact that you had raped Sara until the test results came back. Now we know that it was you who drugged and raped Sara Blake, you who left that knife in Karen's tire, who was making those phone calls, who ran us off the road, who was behind keeping Captain Blake drugged and who injected his IV with a lethal dose of morphine. We had to review the footage from the outside cameras at the hospital. It took a couple of days to get a subpoena to get the security tapes. It was clearly you who snuck in and out of that window."

Karen turned back to Mike.

"Wait! There were two samples found on Sara. Who was the other one?"

"Arthur's. You see, I had Bill take a sample on Arthur too. Sara and her husband had made love that morning right before he left. She was raped only once. And that rapist was you, Major."

Major Murphy frowned at Mike.

"Well, I guess you have it all figured out, don't you?"

"Major, put down the gun. There's no way out of this for you now. It's over." Mike said. He slowly reached for his gun. Major Murphy saw him.

"I wouldn't do that if I were you. It wouldn't be very smart. He pointed his gun from Amanda over to Karen. "Oh, I doubt I'll be spending much time in the brig. You wouldn't believe what strings I can pull. That evidence you have will accidently go missing once I make some calls. You will have nothing on me!" He looked down at Karen. "Now your girlfriend will be dead faster than you could draw your gun. Her death will be your fault. So, you are in a bit of a jam here."

Mike stopped his hand from reaching for the gun.

"You would have had 3 innocent men be convicted for a crime that you committed? Three Marines who looked up to you, trusted you?" Mike asked him.

"In a heartbeat. It's a great feeling to be the one in control. To tell these boys when to jump and how high and have them comply. I could get them promoted quickly or demoted with the connections I have and they respect me for it. I can get these boys to do anything for me; even stay silent for me, at least for a while. Isn't that right Amanda?"

The poor girl was terrified. She was too afraid to move, or even breathe wrong.

"Now move your hand away from your side detective and put both of them in the air."

Slowly, Mike did as he said.

"Very good." Major Murphy said.

He walked over to Mike, still holding the gun, he pointed it at Mike. He reached into Mike's pocket and took the gun out and threw it across the room, but he threw it a little too hard and it went flying out the window to his left. Amanda tried to move closer to the door, but Major Murphy grabbed her and pushed her up against the wall, knocking her out cold. Still holding onto the gun, he quickly grabbed Karen and held the gun to her side.

"Now don't start running or she dies. You don't want to be the cause of your girlfriend's death now, do you, detective?"

Mike was waiting for a chance to pounce. But he knew Karen was in too much danger for him to act just yet. The Major wasn't in a state to negotiate anything with.

Karen was shaking. She was terrified. The gun was against her side. She knew that if she had any chance at all at surviving, she had to get that gun. Just then, there was a noise outside the window. The Major turned around. That was just enough to give Karen the courage and time she needed. She leaned over and knocked the gun out of Major Murphy's hand and ran forward. Mike then lunged forward and grabbed for the gun, but Major Murphy was closer and they both reached down and touched the gun at the same time. There was a struggle and both men were trying to get control of the gun. Major Murphy punched Mike to the floor. Major Murphy now had the gun. He lifted up the gun, aimed it at Karen. She gasped. There was a loud explosion. The room grew silent. Mike looked at Karen. Her facial expression was that of shock and confusion. He asked if she was okay. She looked at her chest. "Yeah, I think so. They both looked at Major Murphy who was still standing with the gun pointed at Karen. His expression was blank. Locked and unchanged. The gun in his hand dropped to the floor, a moment later, so did Major Murphy, with a bullet hole through his chest.

In the window by where Major Murphy had been standing was Arthur, holding a gun. His expression was that of anger and satisfaction. "Easiest quick decision I ever made, you son of a bitch!" He said as he looked down at the body of Major Murphy.

Karen ran over to Amanda and squatted next to her to see if she was okay. Amanda was just coming to when the shot was fired. "What happened? Are you guys okay?" Amanda sat up slowly as she held her head. It was hurting from where she hit the wall. Karen looked over at Arthur, who was climbing through the open window into the room.

"Arthur, how did you know to come here?" Mike asked.

Arthur stood there, never taking his eyes off the body of Major Murphy. He still had the gun pointing to him. Then he spoke up. "I figured out it was Major Murphy when my head finally cleared up. He had been keeping me drugged up so I couldn't think. He had a thing for Sara. I could tell every time he was around her. As my head cleared more from coming off the drugs I was being kept under, I remembered seeing the same film container he had taken from Steven's locker in the Major's car the day I left for Japan. He gave me a ride to the flight terminal that morning. It was in his glove compartment. He closed the door to the glove compartment just as I sat down in the car. He didn't think I saw it but I did. I had forgotten all about it until this morning. He had it the whole time and made us all think that it was missing.

This morning Amanda came to visit me. She told me all that happened at the party. She told me about seeing the film container in his hand as he handed Sara her drink. She told me about how she had gone over to his house to sleep with him and secretly get the sample and turned it in for testing. I then told her about how I had seen the film container in Major Murphy's car that morning. I asked Amanda to be careful because I knew the Major was now a threat. I was still being kept in my hospital room. Major Murphy was here quite a bit today. I guess maybe he heard me and Amanda's conversation somehow, or at least put the pieces together when he saw her come visit me. I believe he was pulling strings and was having the nurses keep me sedated. So, when no one was looking, I knew that I had to get to her house to see if she made it there okay. I knew he might be out to silence all of you before the test results could be made public. I quickly got dressed and snuck out while the nurse stepped away.

Outside, I ran into Bill, who was actually on his way to see me. He had the results of the sample he got from me a couple of days ago when you had brought him to the hospital to meet me. I asked him for a ride here. On the way, he told me the results of my test, that one of the samples was in fact mine. I asked him who the other sample belonged to. He didn't want to tell me at first, some legality BS. but once I put the pressure on and explained how much danger Amanda could be in, he broke down and told me the results. He told me it was Major Murphy's. He was the one who raped Sara. When we arrived here, we parked down a few houses. We thought that if he were here, that we needed to stay low. I told him to call the police when I saw Major Murphy's car parked across the street. So, as I quietly walked up to the house, I heard everything going on inside through this open window. I saw the gun fly out the window and I quickly grabbed it off the ground. When I saw he had a gun pointed to Amanda, I knew I had to act fast. But I couldn't take a shot with her so close to him. But when he threw her down and grabbed

Karen, I aimed and waited til I had a clear shot. I quickly made a noise to distract him. When he turned, luckily Karen was able to get away from him. After Mike and him struggled over the gun I had a moment of a clear shot. So, I pulled the trigger."

"I called the police like you asked me to." Bill said as he entered the room with a few police officers

"Well, it seems that they're on time, as usual." Mike said with a smile.

Mike explained the situation to the officers and everyone was questioned as the body of Major Murphy was taken away by ambulance. A moment later Karen got a call from Ann.

"Mom, what happened?"

"Long story, but I will explain it all in a while. We have some paperwork to go through but in the morning, we should be able to go pick him up."

"Pick who up?" Ann asked with confusion.

"A completely innocent man who will soon be free to help raise my grandchild!" said Karen with a smile.

Ann, Karen, Mike and Arthur stood outside the gate of the brig on base waiting for Josh to be released. The gate opened and he emerged. Ann ran into his arms. They embraced and kissed each other. Mike and Karen smiled at each other as he put his arm around her.

"Well, we sure do work well as a team don't we?" he asked her.

She turned her gaze from Ann and Josh and looked up at Mike.

"We? But you're the one who figured out that it was Major Murphy before I did. I don't know how you figured out how it all happened."

He smiled at her. "That's why I'm a good CID agent."

"That's why you're an excellent CID agent! Jake would be proud."

"Jake would be proud of both of us."

They both looked back at the happy couple being reunited and Mike stroked Karen's cheek.

"I'm so glad that my grandchild will have both his parents raising him." She said. Josh walked over to Karen. "Thank you! You didn't give up on me. That means a lot"

She smiled at him. "You're welcome! She hugged him. Then Josh shook Mike's hand.

Josh and Ann walked arm in arm over to where Stevens, Quinn and Arthur were waiting by some parked cars.

Arthur looked at Josh. For a moment, they locked gazes. Josh didn't know how Arthur would react to him. He was prepared to be punched by Arthur. "Karen told me about Sara kissing you."

Josh looked down at the ground, then back to Arthur. "Man, I am truly sorry for that. I tried to be there for her, make sure she was okay. She thought I was you. I feel so bad! I was your best friend."

"You're wrong." Arthur said. He made a fist. Josh closed his eyes anticipating a punch. But instead, Arthur put his fist up in the air in front of Josh. "You are my best friend."

Josh opened his eyes. Arthur gave Josh a big smile. Josh smiled back and they bumped fists in a gesture of friendship. Then they gave each other a hug.

"Thanks for not hating me, Man." Josh said.

"You didn't hurt her; you were there for her. Man, I could never hate you."

Stevens and Quinn walked up to the two men hugging.

"Hey man, I hope you won't be mad at us for doubting you a little." Quinn said to Josh.

"Yeah, we were scared, confused ya know?" Stevens added. "We had no idea if any of us would make it out. We were totally wrong for that. Can you forgive us?"

Josh looked at them and then at Arthur. Arthur spoke up. "Go on. Forgive 'em. Friends are pretty good to have around. Especially friends who have your back in the air when you need 'em."

"And on the ground." Josh added.

Chapter Twelve

The air was cool as the wind blew through the trees. Brown and green leaves in a small whirl moved across the cemetery. The sun shone brightly on the grass. There was a peaceful feeling all around. Arthur knelt down in front of Sara's freshly placed tombstone. Josh, Stevens, Quinn, Karen, Mike and Ann all stood behind him. In his hand he held white flowers. He looked up for a moment and noticed his surroundings. It was a beautiful place. Lots of green grass, flowers planted nearby in a small garden by a little pond where ducks were bathing. He took a deep breath and looked back down at her freshly covered grave. He had avenged Sara's killer. Sara could now rest in peace and so could he.

"Sara," he spoke softly, "I didn't get to say goodbye to you, not like I wanted to. I didn't get to tell you one last time that I love you. But you know. You always knew. Being with you the last morning we were together was wonderful. I'm glad to have that as my last memory of you. I love you more than you could have ever known. I know you are around me. Watching me, smiling at me. As long as I live, I will never take off my wedding ring because in my heart we are still married. No one could ever fill the void that will always be in my heart, my life. God must have needed an angel because he took you! I'm not mad at the kiss. I know that it really upset you when I was sent away and I know that you needed comfort. I'm glad that Josh was there for you. I miss you like crazy and I'm not sure how I can go on without you, but knowing that you didn't suffer makes me relieved. I just have to take it one day at a time, and be in the air as much as possible. You know that's when I'm at my happiest. Wait for me, Sara, because someday I'm going to be flying up to you. I'll be along someday, when it's my time and I will hold you so tight! We'll be together forever then. But for now, I'm a Marine, and I have a job to do here!"

He put the flowers on her stone as he stood up. He looked back at all his friends behind him. They were tearing up. Karen was rubbing the wedding ring from her late husband that she kept on a chain around her neck. Arthur's words he spoke to his wife hit home for her. She knew the loss he was feeling. As if Mike could read her mind, he rubbed her shoulders and smiled down at her. She was grateful that God had sent her Mike. She knew she wouldn't have made it through the loss of Jake if it wasn't for him being there for her. She loved him. She knew that he couldn't replace Jake, but he was making her happy again, and she knew that Jake would want his greatest love and his best friend to be together.

Arthur walked up to his friends and Josh put his hand on Arthur's shoulder.

"You alright man?" he asked.

Arthur nodded with a small smile. "I'll be ok. I'm just gonna need some time ya know?"

"We're here for ya, man." said Stevens.

"Yeah, we're all here for ya." Quinn said. We're gonna stick together through this with ya."

Quinn stuck out his hand, Arthur stuck out his and placed it on top of Quinn's. Stevens and Josh put their hands on top in a heap. They all stood there in silence, looking at one another. They each knew that the terrible death of Sara had brought them all closer. They all weren't just friends and co-pilots, they were brothers.

Epilogue

November 14, 2018

The doors of the chapel on base swung open as Josh and Ann stepped out. They were greeted by cheers and flying birdseed. Ann stood holding the bouquet and waving as everyone applauded the happy new married couple. Josh stood in his dress blues and kissed his new bride. Karen and Mike emerged out of the chapel behind them. Mike was wearing a black tuxedo and Karen was in a pink dress, holding a bouquet.

"Congratulations to both couples!" yelled Bill from out of the crowd.

Ann and Karen both turned around and threw their bouquets. Amanda caught one of them.

She turned to the girl next to her and handed her the bouquet. "Not for me! I'm gonna enjoy my freedom as long as I can."

Mike and Josh shook hands while the mother and daughter brides hugged.

Ann turned back to Josh as she rubbed her baby belly. "It's too bad that Arthur, Quinn and Stevens couldn't stay for the reception."

"Yeah, it is too bad." interrupted Karen. "Where are they anyway?"

Mike and Josh just smiled. "Oh, they'll be along shortly!" said Josh.

Karen and Ann just looked puzzled at each other.

Just then they heard the roar of jets in the distance. They all looked up as three jets went flying by low overhead. The 3 pilots dipped their wings as they flew by.

"I told you they would be by shortly." Josh said. "They wanted to give us a proper salute."

Please check out my previously

released book:

All My Love, Martin

About The Author

Julie D'Olympio

Julie has always had a passion for writing. As a young child, she wanted to be a writer. She is the daughter of an Air Force veteran. Her family moved around a lot and she was in a new school almost every year. Writing kept her grounded. At the age of 19 she married her high school sweetheart and moved to California where he was stationed in the Marine Corps. The military has always been a part of her life and is a huge influence on her writing. She lives in Florida with her husband of 28 years. They have a daughter in college. Her family is very important to Julie and they continue to inspire her every day.

9 780578 314426